THE CHRONICLES OF AN OUTRYDER

The Canyon's Edge

CONNOR OSWALD

THE CHRONICLES OF AN OUTRYDER
THE CANYON'S EDGE

iUniverse books may be ordered through booksellers or by contacting:

iUniverse
1663 Liberty Drive
Bloomington, IN 47403
www.iuniverse.com
844-349-9409

Because of the dynamic nature of the Internet, any web addresses or links contained in this book may have changed since publication and may no longer be valid. The views expressed in this work are solely those of the author and do not necessarily reflect the views of the publisher, and the publisher hereby disclaims any responsibility for them.

Any people depicted in stock imagery provided by Getty Images are models, and such images are being used for illustrative purposes only. Certain stock imagery © Getty Images.

ISBN: 978-1-6632-2883-3 (sc)
ISBN: 978-1-6632-2884-0 (e)

Library of Congress Control Number: 2021918892

Print information available on the last page.

iUniverse rev. date: 09/24/2021

Chapter 1

❈

"Anjagor is one of the most powerful nations today, followed in suite by the Galak nation and finally, the nation of Bianet......... Haran wake up please." He snapped awake slamming his head into the stone wall behind him, he looked over to Heide who was covering up her laughter.

"Sorry Lady Usrea," he said rubbing his head, as she looked at him with a piercing glare.

Lady Usrea was a middle aged, kind teacher at the castle Haran lived at, Castle Norhall, one of the most beautiful castles in all Anjagor, with its unique shape being that of a rhombus. As the legend goes, trolls built the castle hundreds of years ago, but most educated people know it was a just drunken designer some 100 years ago. As for the town of Norhall, it is a quiet place, with blacksmiths, bakeries, mills, taverns, houses and an inn. A river that was about three meters wide, called the Wolfs Tail, separated the village from the castle. The inside of the castle was a basic design with a keep in the center and merchant tents along the roads, wells and stables for horses. And finally, the one-room building they called school near the keep where orphaned children of wealthy descent, like Haran, went to learn.

"Haran you better listen, you are going to need it one day... anyway class dismissed everyone get some rest, big day tomorrow," said Lady Usrea. Haran highly doubted he was going to need to know this pointless information for his craft, but since he really didn't know what craft he wanted to do, he paid some attention. Tomorrow was the day that Haran and his classmates would be chosen for a craft to specialize in. After

Haran left the class with his three classmates, Bertrand, Heide, and Lottie he looked over to the three of them. Bertrand was short in stature and slim, and he was always mumbling to his feet even around people he had known his whole life. However, despite the shyness he was extremely smart, and Haran knew he would be chosen for to be a scribe. Heide is tall, elegant, and looked as if she were hand crafted by a goddess of beauty. She was always nice and always tried to figure out a way for Haran and Lottie to coexist peacefully. She would be chosen as a courier to go on diplomatic missions. Lottie towered over all three, a powerful bully, who always wanted to pick a fight with someone, particularly Haran. Lottie would surely be a Norhall knight, for he had been training with a sword since he could carry one. Haran and Lottie have gotten into their fair share of fights over the past few years with Lottie usually coming out on top. However, Haran was fast on his feet and quick witted so sometimes after he had gotten that one last quip in, he would just run away until Lottie tired out.

The four of them were orphans or at least abandoned at a young age, Heide's dad died in the first Frelorian War and her mother died due to childbirth complications. Lottie's father disappeared shortly after he was born, and his mother died of heartbreak. Both of Bertrand's parents died in a fire when he was three. And then Haran who had randomly showed up on the Baron's front door as a baby along with a satchel with a weird, shaped R on it and a note that read, 'Take good care of the boy, his father was born a hero and died as one, his mother was taken in the war with the Frelorians.'

Haran got into the keep, which was up the stairs from the Great Hall, the keep is where the Baron and the orphans stayed. When he got into his room, which had one bed, one place to use the bathroom, one table, two chairs and one fireplace, he put down his satchel given to him by his father.

Soon after, Haran heard shouts from the gate entrance and saw a bloody horseman galloping through the gates. The horse he was on was shaggy and unkempt as if it hadn't been combed in several months; however, the horse had some speed to it. It galloped across the courtyard, leaving a cloud of gravel and dirt in its wake. As the rider got closer to the keep Haran could make out an insignia of three stars in the shape of a triangle connected by vines on the rider's shield, the insignia belonging to the fief of Dalhurst. Dalhurst was a small fief adjacent to the fief Haran was in, Norhall. Norhall was one of the largest fiefs in Anjagor, only second to the Anjagor fief itself. Out of the thirty-five fiefs of Anjagor, Dalhurst was one of the poorest due to its lack of good Baronship as well as its location right next to the Hermirtha Sea. If you lived near the Hermirtha Sea at all you were subject to being raided by savage vikings from the nation of Bianet, and Dalhurst took the heaviest blows when it came to the raids. They get raided almost every year during the summer and spring months and are stuck rebuilding in the fall and winter. A deadly cycle that can kill any growth in a fief.

The bloody rider, after practically jumping off his horse, sprinted into the Great Hall that lead up to the keep. Presumably to talk to the Baron of Norhall fief, Baron Ligate. Baron Ligate was a classic Anjagor native, with a blond hair and blue eyes. He was a general up until a battle a few years back when he lost his leg to a rogue Norhall soldier. He won the title of Baron from the king, and has been here ever since. He was a stern man, something you would expect as a commander for the army, and a master swordsman. However, at least to the kids, he had always had a sense of compassion, after all they were almost like his own children in a way. The Baron did not have kids of his own in between his wife dying in childbirth, and him not wanting to remarry, these kids were all he had.

Haran was intrigued by the mysterious rider, and decided he needed to find out more about what he was in such a rush for. So he decided to take a peak out of his door; his room being right in front of the stairs. But by the time he opened the door, the rider was already in the Baron's quarters. Hours later, Haran heard the mysterious rider leave; he was heading towards Fuestres Woods, a thick forest about a kilometer northeast of Norhall Castle. Haran made a mental note to talk to the Baron about the strange rider from Dalhurst tonight at dinner.

Dinners at Castle Norhall were joyous affairs, with close friends of the Baron and the orphaned children conversing, dancing and eating the massive amount of food the chefs would create. Haran, conversely, was not in a happy mood, something about the soldier from Dalhurst was familiar to him. But before he could think about it too much Heide took his hand, "Come here, sad boy; let's cheer you up," she said as she took him to the dance floor. The dance floor was in the middle of the great hall, with one long table on its right side. When there was a bigger feast, they would bring out more tables, but for the twenty-five people in the room now, one was plenty. As they swayed slowly, Haran found it strange how even now, after all these years, he could still be this deeply in love with the girl. "What is the matter," she said as they swayed looking into each other's eyes. They had known each other for long enough to tell when something was wrong.

"Did you hear all that commotion earlier, right after we left school?" Haran asked thoughts racing through his head of the horse and the rider. Why was he bloody? Why was he in such a hurry? What did he talk to Baron Ligate about?

"Yeah, a messenger, from Dalhurst I think. But what does that got to do with anything? Ligate gets messengers all the time." Heide said as she looked into his eyes, never daring to break contact.

"Well, I just feel I have seen the man before, or felt his presence at least," he responded looking into her crystal blue eyes, and her red flowing hair, and he lost himself, lost all his worries in a matter of seconds.

Before she could respond Baron Ligate bellowed, "I think it's time for a toast," which startled Haran. The Baron waited for everyone to find their seats then gestured for the children to stand. His voice boomed across the hall, the sound of a commander in the middle of a battle, "Tomorrow, Norhall's finest children are being selected to serve the nation as productive citizens, either as knights who will protect this kingdom till death do them part, or as a blacksmith who provide people with weapons for these knights. Or as a scribe to help make contracts and treaties, or as a courier who is to deliver and negotiate these said treaties. I ask you tonight to look to the future, and it is here," he said waving his arms to the four children.

There was a resounding applause from everyone in the room as all the children turned ruby red. As the cheers died down, Haran saw the Baron exit quietly through the side door, and he silently cursed to himself. He had been hoping to talk to him. He got up to go after him, but as he got up, he accidentally hit Lottie, who was walking by, "What is your problem pipsqueak," Lottie asked slurring his words because he had drunk a little too much ale.

"Nothing, ale brain It was an accident," Haran replied. Knowing Lottie always hated when his intellect was mentioned.

"What did you just call me," Lottie asked a little louder.

"Oh yeah, I forgot who I was talking to let me spell it out for you A-L-E-B-R-A-I-N," Haran said in a slow mocking tone. One that you would take if talking to a young child who just can't pronounce a word. Lottie was furious, so furious that he tried to strike Haran. However, Haran was quick, and Lottie had been drinking so Haran easily dodged it. But, as he was running for the door to the courtyard Lottie tackled him, slamming him against the rock wall. Lottie reared back his fist getting ready to throw a punch when a guard yanked him off of Haran. A crowd had amassed behind the angry boys.

"If this is our finest, this whole nation is doomed," the first guard said, as a second guard scoffed and shoed the crowd that had built up away.

Haran went straight to his room angrily, putting all his weight on each step, thinking maybe he could just break one if he stepped hard enough. Heide followed him; however, she was graceful in her approach, "He could have killed you Haran! What were you thinking?" she asked furiously as she went up the steps behind him.

"Well someone has to shut him up one day Heide," Haran said wincing as he moved because Lottie slammed him into a protruding rock during their altercation.

"Well, you can't do it Haran I don't want you to get hurt, he will get his day one day just not today, and that can't be the only thing bugging you," said Heide compassionately.

"Well," Haran admitted, "I guess I was kind of annoyed that I didn't have a chance to speak to the Baron about that rider this morning, and I was taking my anger out on Lottie."

"Ok, well I'm sorry that you didn't get to talk to the Baron, but there is always tomorrow, and tonight you need sleep," said Heide as she walked down the hall and into her room down the hall. Haran went inside his room, but he knew he could not sleep thinking of the day to come and pondering over the path he could be chosen for. He would have liked to be a blacksmith, but Udo, the best blacksmith in the fief of Norhall, had already taken on three apprentices last year and all his spots were filled. As these thoughts raced through his mind, he heard something just outside the castle wall, something so minuscule that most people would have thought was the wind. However, Haran was not like most people, for his ears were trained due to him sitting every night at his window. He just sat listening to the gentle breeze, the chirping insects and the occasional movement from guards. This sound, this was different, it was more of a scratching sound on the stone walls outside the castle, a scratch then a thump on the ground, scratch, thump, scratch, thump, scratch. Haran contemplated going to investigate the noise, then he made up his mind, "Nothing better to do I guess," he whispered as climbed out of his window and down the keep wall into the courtyard with little to no sound as he worked his way to the outer wall of the castle. He picked up a large rock from the gravel road and stuffed it into his satchel, a possible distraction. He had snuck out many times before, and after he got caught the first few times, he knew when the guards changed their shifts, and that time was now. He climbed his way slowly up the southwest wall trying to time him getting to the top to when the guards changed. Some guards left, but a few stayed their post until their relievers arrive. The guards who remained did not seem to hear the sound from earlier, and if they did they probably just passed it off as the wind rustling the leaves in the distance. Haran peaked his head over the ramparts slightly to check if there were any guards left, there was one on the southeast wall which faces the Malen Plains, a plains three kilometers in distance of just tall grass. Malen Plains also contains the Battleschool which is where young men from their respective fiefs go to be fully knighted and serve the kingdom of Anjagor. Many guards don't expect any trouble from the southwest wall because it would be virtual suicide to have an army come from the plains.

There were two guards on the northwest wall, which was the wall facing the village and the Wolf's Tail. Four guards on the northeast wall because that is the direction of the Fuestres Woods, the most likely direction of attack. However, Haran had heard the sounds from the southwest wall, the wall closest to his room, and the wall that faced the Calcore Canyon. Calcore Canyon was a canyon about fifty meters wide, and one hundred and fifty meters deep. Like most canyons, Calcore was dry and full of jetting orange rocks and sand. Unlike much of Norhall which was filled with rich, vibrant greens and yellows. The canyon had tiny caves scattered throughout the bottom and middle full of ravenous wolves at the bottom, and terrifying vultures in the middle. Haran never dared to explore the canyon at night, for they had found many bodies in the bottom of that canyon. The southwest wall had one guard on it, who was about 3 meters away from Haran and about to turn to face him. Haran always had his satchel, once belonging to his father, and the only thing that reminded Haran of his parents. The rock that he put in the satchel, he now planned to use it divert the guard's attention. Haran sent the rock tumbling down the street into the courtyard below the guard looked to the ground below hearing the noise and checked all around him to find nothing. Haran slipped by the unaware guard and made his way down the castle wall, easily being able to climb to the ground with little to no noise at all.

At the bottom of the wall, Haran looked for close to two hours going back and forth… then it started raining and that is when the thought occurred to him. There was a chunk of the wall around three meters up the wall that was missing from the Athons siege ten years back that has still not been fixed. Maybe whatever it was went up there to seek shelter.

The Athons were generally peaceful polytheistic people; however, ten years ago an unruly, power-hungry king, King

Werneck took over the throne and decided that he was going to invade Anjagor. After they made it through the Ediv Pass (the only way to Anjagor from Athon without ships) the Athons leveled many fiefs on their way to the capital. However, when they made it to Norhall they were stopped by the Outryder of this fief, Orion, and the knights of Norhall.

He thought he could check the hole, maybe whatever it was that made the sound was searching for shelter for the night and protection from the rain. As he climbed higher, he heard what sounded like a tiny animal in pain, and as he looked where the missing chunk of the wall was, he saw it. A mysterious catlike creature, but it was already the size of a regular cat when it looked to be only a month or so old; it was fluffy and dark yellow with little black dots on his forehead. The creature was scared and looked as if it had not eaten in days, it backed away from Haran as he started to pet it. So he took out the piece of bread he from his satchel and put it in front of the cat. The creature let out a high-pitched call and took the bread gratefully. He noticed that the creature's hind paws had been hurt when it limped to the food. Haran figured that the sounds he heard were the cat falling to the ground from this height and climbing back up. Haran picked up the cat who had gotten accustom to him now and put it in his satchel. Then he climbed into the hole and waited until morning when he could walk straight through the gates.

Chapter 2

After getting back into his room the following morning he let his new friend out of the satchel, it was the big day today and he had hardly gotten sleep last night. "Wait here I'll be back in a few hours," he said to the creature who just looked at him curiously. After standing at the entrance of Haran's room for a few seconds, it went over next to the fire and plopped itself there, slowly drifting off to sleep.

As Haran exited the door, he locked it behind him as to not let anyone discover his new pet. "Why lock your door?" Heide asked quizzically, startling Haran. He hated lying to Heide, but he would explain everything later. "No reason," he lied, "Anyway ready for the big day?" Haran said hiding his key in his satchel.

Heide responded, "Ready as I'll ever be," as they went down the hall to the Baron's chamber. Lottie and Bertrand were already waiting outside the door when Haran and Heide walked up. Barte opened the door to let them in; Barte was Baron Ligate's assistant, short and stocky, he reminded Haran of a pig. And even though he looked like a pig, he carried himself as if he were a king which earned the slightest bit of Haran's respect, "Is everyone here...One...Two...Three... Four... ok great." They all walked in the Baron's quarters and were amazed at how simple it was, they were expecting extravagant chandeliers, finely woven tapestries and beautifully crafted furniture. Instead, there was just four chairs next to a fireplace, a dining table, and a bed, the same as everyone else's rooms. The only thing different was an extra room where the Baron's office was. As they all walked in and got adjusted accordingly, Haran saw Barte walk over to Baron Ligate and hand him a note. As Barte handed the note to the Baron he spoke in a low tone, so low that Haran could only make out the words "Dalhurst" and "messenger". Haran perked up trying to listen for more information, but to no avail. Haran knew there was something in that note about the mysterious rider from Dalhurst and he also knew that he could not rest until he knew what it was.

"Good morning children," Ligate said after he put the note on his desk, "So today you will be chosen to be apprenticed by a master and to do that you must be tested."

There was a litany of questions that rang out from the four children. "Tested??" Bertrand asked. "What do you mean tested?" Heide said. "What kind of test?" asked Haran.

"Calm down children and wait for me to explain," said the Baron, the children got quiet, and the Baron continued, "Today you will be tested on your knowledge, and your athleticism. For the knowledge portion you will take a quiz to test your basic knowledge and your knowledge of Anjagor. For the athleticism you will be told to finish a difficult obstacle course, followed by a footrace. The masters will be watching every test. Any questions?"

The children shook their heads no, "Ok, so you will be taking your knowledge test in fifteen minutes in your classroom," He finished, waving the children out of his quarters. As the children headed to their classroom Haran was already devising a plan to sneak into the Baron's office and see what was on that note.

The knowledge test was like any other test, you went in, sat down and took the test, but this test was a little different because it was over everything that Lady Usrea had ever taught them. Haran knew that Heide and Bertrand were going to do well on it, and Haran himself would do well on the basic knowledge portion, but he knew Lottie never paid attention and was not very sharp.

The test started with a short answer question, "Who were the Lupens?" Haran remembered this lesson vaguely, they were ruthless barbarians who once lived in the Norhall fief, but they were run out by Outin Ryder, the first Outryder. He wrote that and moved on to the next question.

And the last question on the test asked, "What are the three greatest nations in the world today in order from greatest to least _____, _____, and _____?" He silently cursed under his breath, knowing he had slept right through this lesson.

Haran put "Anjagor ? and ?" and turned his test in to Lady Usrea.

As they were exiting the school after the knowledge test, Baron Ligate told the four children to meet him in the Malen Plains right outside of the castle. When they got there, they were shocked, as there was an obstacle course 100 meters long with ramps, ropes, walls, and mud, all seemingly increasingly harder to get past.

"When did you make this," asked Haran for he had been in this area the day before yesterday and did not see anyone working on it.

Heide whispered to him, "It is a lot of different pieces that they bring out every time they are testing kids like us. The last time they brought it out was 2 years ago with those orphans and now they brought it out for us." After she said that, they realized when they are going to have to get to the end of this obstacle course while being judged along the way. As Haran looked over to the masters, he caught a glimpse at someone he had seen only once before, Orion, and it sent shivers down his spine.

Orion was one of the most renown members of the Outryders. These Outryders were a secretive group of deadly warriors who fought for Anjagor dressed in weird greenish cloak with a sash of throwing knives over it. It is rumored that these Outryders kill you with just a simple gaze, and their most foremost member was staring Haran dead in his eyes. Even though he was this far from the Outryder, he felt fear, for his eyes were steely and dark like Haran was staring into darkness itself.

"After you finish the obstacle course you will race all the way back to this location. Understand?" asked Baron Ligate. The children all nodded and got ready to do the course, "Ok then, Three...Two...One...Go."

The children took off with Haran taking the early lead, followed by Lottie, Heide and Bertrand. As Haran got to the first wall, he scaled it with relative ease, and moved onto the rope climb. Here is where Lottie caught back up reaching the top and ringing the bell a couple seconds before Haran. Past the rope climb, there was a ramp you had to run up and jump off to catch a rope where swing to more ropes down the line; Lottie took a more sizable lead here, but Haran held his own. With Lottie in the lead by a decent margin, Haran in second, and Heide and Bertrand still on the swinging ropes, Haran climbed the last wall and reached the final ten meters the mud crawl. The mud crawl was probably the hardest of all of the obstacles because there were ropes suspended about a half a meter from the ground and as the master scribe, Conrad, pointed out when Haran got there, "If you touch the ropes at all you must go back to the start of the mud."

Lottie was halfway through when his back scraped against the ropes, "GO BACK LOTTIE!" Conrad yelled.

With Lottie having to go all the way back to the start he thought there was no way he could catch up, but at about six meters in Haran had also scraped his back on the ropes. "HARAN YOU TOO!"

When Haran got back to the start of the mud crawl, Lottie was halfway through and he saw Heide and Bertrand running to the mud crawl now, he started on his way and halfway through, he saw that Lottie had finished and was running back to the start. When Haran got out of the mud, he saw that Lottie was already fifteen meters in, and he took off after him, gaining slowly, wondering if it was going to be enough to catch up. About five meters to the finish, Lottie looked back to see Haran right on his tail. Haran, about to overtake the bigger boy saw that Lottie had changed his stride with Haran right behind him. Haran could not move clear fast enough, so his foot caught Lottie's and he fell, tumbling and injuring his already hurt ribs on a rock hidden in the long grass. As Lottie finished, Haran got up and finished the rest of the run clutching his side the rest of the way.

"Aww what happened to the wittle baby," said Lottie in a mocking tone knowing full well what he did.

Haran was furious knowing he would have beat Lottie if the boy had not cheated, "What is your problem," Haran said to Lottie. "It's not like you to be scared of a little competition, oh wait it is when you know you're going to lose." Haran said mockingly.

"I wasn't going to lose to you pipsqueak and I aint scared of nothing," Lottie said as he got right into Haran's face.

The tension broke when Heide showed up, followed shortly by Bertrand, "Ok, stop the bickering you two," said Baron Ligate and the boys broke off. Heide looked worriedly over to Haran who refused to meet her eye.

After about thirty seconds Baron Ligate finally spoke, "Alright boys and girl why don't you get cleaned up and enjoy the rest of your day, you will be contacted by your respective masters within a few days." As everyone went their separate ways, some townsfolk started taking down the obstacle course.

Haran had planned to explore a cave near the bottom of Calcore Canyon, but he did not think he could scale those walls with his ribs in the shape they were in.

As he tried to open his room door, he remembered that he had locked it because of the weird creature he had found the night before. So, he took out his key from his satchel, unlocked the door, and opened it, when he saw the peculiar looking cat still there sound asleep next to the fireplace. He had not really thought about it, but now that he did, Haran remembered something Lady Usrea taught them something about big cats. He also knew that cats were supposed to be evil, vial creatures who were associated with witchcraft, but this one seemed calm, playful, even nice.

"How about I go find out what you really are," he said to the sleeping cat as he headed off to find Lady Usrea. He first looked in the classroom, then her quarters, and finally found her in the library reading a book titled *The Rich History of Anjagor.*

As he approached her, she looked up from her book and said, "Hey Haran, how can I help you?"

He responded almost immediately, "Hey Lady Usrea, I was just wondering, do you know of any big catlike creatures that could be in Anjagor," Haran asked.

Lady Usrea looked at him quizzically for a couple seconds, then finally responded, "I don't know of any big catlike creature in Anjagor no, but there are three different types in the plains of Afros." Haran had a puzzled look on his face, he had heard of the name before, she saw him struggling and answered her own unasked question, "Ahh yet another lesson you slept through, Afros is a land of warring tribes coveting power over one another with a lack of cohesion or decisive winners and losers. It is across the Hermirtha Sea to the southwest, but I don't know how one of those cats could be in Anjagor."

15

"What do the three cats look like," Haran asked. Lady Usrea got up and after a minute, she came back with a book that read *The Ecosystems of Afros*.

She read it for a minute and said, "It says here that the biggest one is called a lion which is built to hunt big creatures, it is pure muscle, and they appear to have long, shaggy manes and pure yellow coats. The lion cubs usually have tiny black spots especially around their head. The next one is called a cheetah, apparently lean, yet strong and it says here that they can run faster than anything that the writer had seen and have small black spots on their yellow coats. And finally, the leopards the smallest big cat in height, they are like cheetahs but slower, and appear heavier set than cheetahs, they also have a yellow coat but instead of tiny black dots on a cheetah, leopards have bigger black shapes on their coats."

Haran, taking in all this information now knew exactly what his little friend was… Haran found a lion.

As he got back to his room, he had to push his little lion friend out of his mind, due to him having to go eat dinner. The baby lion popped his head up curious at where his new owner was going, "Don't worry I'll bring you something to eat." Haran said as he exited the room.

Dinner was the usual affair, eating, drinking, music and dancing, and as they finished eating Haran saw him again out of the corner of his eye, the mysterious Orion, handing Baron Ligate what looked like a shield with Dalhurst's insignia on it. "What is going on," he said to himself as he saw the exchange. Haran returned to his room early with some mutton from the dinner. He set it on the floor near his new lion friend, he devised a plan to get into Baron Ligate's office to look at the note given to him that morning and put to rest all his speculation about the mysterious rider from Dalhurst.

Chapter 3

It was half past eleven when his plan started; part one was already on the way as he had paid one to the younger children of the keep a bag of silvers to cause a distraction that woke everyone up and got them out of their bed. Haran had given this kid a small horn and told him to blow it till he could not breathe at exactly thirty minutes after eleven. That time was now, as he heard the horn blast from the empty courtyard below. Heard it echo, bouncing off the castle walls and ringing just loud enough to wake everyone in the keep up. If he had given this task to a man, they would have surely woken up the entire village bellow.

As everyone left their rooms to see what that awful sound was, Haran peaked his head out of his door just in time to see the Baron walking down the stairs to see what was going on. Haran knew they would soon find the kid, so he knew he had only a little time to get into Baron Ligate's office. Haran waited until the halls were completely empty, and he sprinted off to the Baron's quarters. As he got there, he found the door unlocked, exactly what he had hoped for, he crept in the Baron's office, he picked up the note sitting right on the desk, opened it to find that it just said three words. "Look behind you." As he looked back a hand came out of the darkness, gripping Haran's wrist not letting him escape. Panic washed over Haran, he was caught, but by who.

"Care to explain yourself," Haran heard the owner of the hand say in a steely, cold voice.

It was just at this time that Baron Ligate came into his office with a torch lighting up the strange shadowy figure that was now illuminated.

Haran was petrified to be standing only a meter from the legend Orion, and safe to say he was not impressed; Orion was a head shorter than the Baron and at least 20 kilograms lighter. However, Haran somehow knew if the two were to ever fight, Orion would win. He could tell this not by his legendary persona or by the way he carried himself, but from his eyes, for they were grey, cold and sharp like daggers, somehow piercing their way into Haran's very soul. This was no man to mess with; Orion let go of Haran's wrist, but he could still feel where Orion's hand once locked to it.

"Explain yourself" said Ligate coldly, but with a hint of compassion for the young boy.

Haran responded, speaking so fast it was almost incomprehensible, "I'm sorry Baron I just really wanted to know about that rider from Dalhurst from the other day I know I should have asked you, but I knew you would not tell me, and I'm sorry for setting up that elaborate ruse to distract yo...."

Ligate stopped him before he could go any further, "I know child, I know, and I hope you know how irresponsible it was sneaking into my quarters in the middle of the night."

Haran nodded and said, "Yes Baron, I know, but I was just so curious about that rider, he looked familiar to me."

Ligate replied "You really want to know who it was?" Haran nodded and the Baron pointed to the Outryder standing in the corner of the room, "It was Orion here."

"You? But I do not understand, why would you do that?" Haran asked, addressing Orion.

"Well," said Ligate, "It was actually all for you, he suggested that he ride into the castle, bloody, with the guise of a knight from Dalhurst to stir up your natural sense of curiosity. And he knew, somehow, that if you saw Barte hand me a note and heard him talking to me about a rider from Dalhurst that you would try to get us out of the room so that you could steal the note."

Haran was visibly shook, he had so many questions, but he started off with just off with just one, "How did you know that I would try and look at the note?"

Orion responded, "Well Haran I have been watching you for years now, I have seen you exploring everything interesting in this fief since you were old enough to walk so, I knew that you would try and look at the note and I also know about the baby cheetah that you rescued from the hole in the wall the other night."

Haran corrected him almost immediately, "It is actually a lion, cheetahs have small dark spots, while lions…." he stopped as Orion had given him a spine-chilling gaze.

Haran still had one more question though, "Why me, what makes me so important for you all to go through this much effort to get me here?"

"Well Haran," said Ligate, "We put in this much effort to tell you that Orion is hoping to recruit you, to be a part of the Outryders."

Haran's jaw gaped open as he heard the name, him as an Outryder, he just couldn't believe it, "Wha, wha, what does that mean the Outryders?" he asked, shocked by the request.

"Well, you won't start out as a full-blown Outryder of course, you would be training under Orion as a Recon, or Outryder's apprentice, until he deems you worthy of the Outryder title," Ligate paused waiting for a response.

"Are you serious?" asked Haran thinking this was all a dream.

Litgate looked at Orion and back to Haran responding, "Yes son if you agree you begin a whole new chapter in your life, however it is a dangerous one. Outryders are the most skilled warriors in all of Anjagor, which means that you will face many challenges internally and externally. However, I do respect and trust Orion with my life and he is ready to take you as his Recon, are you ready?"

"Of course," said Haran excitedly bouncing up and down on his toes," When do I start?"

This time Orion responded, "Tomorrow at sunrise I will be at the stables with a packhorse so take all your belongings and be there by the time I get there, or you will regret making me wait."

As Haran exited the Baron's quarters, he ran into Heide on her way back to her room and explained everything that had just happened to him, "The Outryders?" she asked, her eyes getting wider and her face more worried. As most knew, the Outryders were known for their mysterious ways.

"I will be fine, Baron Ligate reassured me that he trusts Orion with his life, and he wouldn't let me join if he didn't." said Haran reassuringly.

"Ok well great," Heide said as she looked worriedly into Haran's eyes.

"And, did Anna approach you yet," Haran asked. Anna was the master courier in Norhall, tall and graceful as was Heide, she oversaw all transport of messages into and out of Norhall, there was almost nothing she didn't know about the inner workings of each fief. And Haran was aware that Heide had always looked up to her as a role model and personal hero.

"Yes. Shortly after you left she asked me to be apart of her couriers, I start tomorrow,"

"Well that's fantastic," he knew it would happen, but he was happy for he nonetheless, "And what of Lottie and Bertrand?" Haran asked curiously.

"Well, master Scribe Conrad asked Bertrand to be his apprentice while he was leaving dinner and Battlemaster Gilpin took Lottie under his wing," Heide said.

Gilpin ran the Battleschool in Norhall, a training ground for knight's apprentices that help raise a new round of trained warriors for the Norhall fief. "Both obvious choices of course, anyway when are we to see each other again," Haran asked with a hint of sadness in his eye, knowing they each were going their separate ways.

"Well," she responded pondering the next time they would all be together, "When we have the annual festival on the winter solstice, it's in about 4 months," Heide said.

"Ok, well I will make sure I am there," Haran promised.

"You'd better," Heide said punching him in the arm. He laughed and was about to walk away, but before turned to leave, she gave him a kiss farewell, at least for a little while. As Haran returned to his room, the warm feeling still remained and he was left wondering what had just happened.

Chapter 4

❁

Haran had taken Orion's warning to heart and got a good night's sleep. He did not have much to pack other than some changes of clothes, his satchel, some food, and of course his new friend, the baby lion. He got to the stables thirty minutes before sunrise and not a minute later, that's when he saw Orion already standing at a stable with the packhorse he promised. "You told me you would be here at sunrise, why are you here so early?" Haran asked skeptically.

"First lesson. don't ask stupid questions, I showed up early to make sure you were on your game, and you were so let us get going," said Orion blankly.

As they walked through the town, Haran heard whispers of "Outryder" and "Magic" from inside the houses. "You don't actually do magic, do you? The Outryders I mean," asked Haran curiously, he had always heard Outryders were ones of supernatural abilities, but Orion didn't seem as such.

Orion fell quiet at the question as they walked out the gates and then responded with a simple, "Depends who you ask, if you ask the townsfolk, it's a yes, but if you ask anyone who has ever actually talked to an Outryder, the answer is no."

Haran was confused, but he was fairly sure that meant no, and continued to follow his new master. They walked side by side down the dirt road a few kilometers Haran not daring to ask another question. They were almost in Fuestres Woods when Haran asked, "What are we doing here?"

Orion was silent, so Haran continued, "I have never really explored to far into here, it's just so confusing, all the tree and winding trails, I could never really map it out fully."

"That's the point" Orion said, his eyes darting from side to side as if he were looking for something.

"Hey, I have been meaning to ask…" he trailed off as Orion held his hand up to stop, that's when he heard, a tiny screech coming from the pack horse behind him. Orion knew immediately what it was, "You brought the cheetah," he asked rhetorically.

"Oh yes, I have been meaning to ask you can I keep the lion at wherever we are going," Haran said emphasizing lion. Orion continued walking, going through all the winding trails of Fuestres Woods, yet he still seemed to know his bearings.

Orion took a deep breath, "I suppose, Lyra already has her dog so it would only be fair to let you have your cat."

"Who is Lyra?" Haran asked, thinking he would be the only Recon training under Orion.

Orion responded with, "Just see for yourself." As they turned a corner, he saw it, a beautiful clearing about two hundred meters in diameter with perfectly cut grass and a sizable log cabin in the center. To the left of the cabin there looked to be a stable and to the right at the very edge of the clearing, a crystal blue spring that looked very delightful in the late summer weather.

Orion stopped in front of the cabin with the packhorse, "Unpack your stuff" he said as he walked into the cabin leaving Haran outside to unpack and bring his stuff inside. After taking all his stuff off of the packhorse he walked into the cabin where to the right he saw a fireplace stoked and burning, with three chairs and a table beside it, he also saw a little kitchen area and a hallway that led to what looked like four rooms. Haran had guessed one would be for him, one for Orion to sleep, one office, and one for the unknown Lyra.

Orion picked up some papers from the table and said, "Have Lyra show you around I have got a letter from the king to read," as he went into the first room and shut the door behind him. Haran dropped his stuff on the ground near the door and went to go check out his new home. He had known the second room was Orion's due to the door he saw in his office connecting the two, so he checked the third TAP-TAP. Before he could do the third and final knock the door opened, and he saw a girl. She was a beautiful girl with long dark hair and dark brown eyes she was very pretty, but she didn't look like she was from Anjagor, her skin was tanned from exposure to the sun, and most natives have either blond or red hair. Haran himself had darker blond hair bordering on brown, but his eyes were those of natives, sea green.

"Ah it's you," she said feigning enthusiasm.

Haran spoke, a little too eager, "I'm Haran, and you must be Lyra."

She looked uninterested already and just let out a simple, "Follow me," as she walked by him briskly.

When they got outside Lyra whistled and an orange, small wolf-like creature came running out of the wood seconds later, Haran looked at it curiously wondering what it was, "Scarlett is a fox" she said somehow knowing what he was thinking, "I bet Orion called her a dog huh." Haran responded with a simple head nod, she scoffed, "Of course he did. Well let me show you around," she said walking toward spring.

"This right here is the spring this is where we get all of our water for bathing, washing clothes and drinking," Lyra paused gesturing toward the spring, then she continued going to the backside of the cabin.

There were wooden human sized targets at varying distances and a sand pit for combat, "This here is the training grounds this is where you and I will train everyday under the close eyes of Orion, but you won't be training here at first," she said as one off and continued to the stables.

"What will I be doing?" Haran asked wanting to get started as fast as possible.

"Oh, you'll see" she said with a slight smile which Haran did not take that as a good sign. "And finally the stables, where we keep our horses," she finished, Haran was about to ask where his horse was then he remembered the first lesson, "Don't ask stupid questions."

"Alright, go unpack your stuff, then tell Orion that you are ready to start," she said looking at his handsomely rugged face and his sea green eyes.

As he went into the cabin with all his stuff and started to unpack, he took out a painting of Heide and himself she got him for his birthday last year and hung it on the wall, as he whispered silently "four more months."

Chapter 5

His first few days were awful, Orion had made him go through a rigorous process, that seemed to have no purpose. The first three days he had set him on a ridiculous task to move buckets full of heavy rocks from Calcore Canyon, which was six kilometers from the forest to the spring to "keep the spring balanced," Orion had said, whatever that meant. On the fourth day, Orion had taken him to a fallen tree that was a meter is diameter and about 30 meters in length in the middle of a small game trail.

"Open the trail by sunset or you will be back on rock duty," said Orion stone-faced.

"How am I supposed to do that," Haran asked skeptically.

Orion shrugged and said, "Not my problem," as he reached behind his back and took one of his axes out and threw it on the ground in front of Haran him.

Haran pondered how he would get the giant tree out of the way, he could have tried to cut up, but that would take five days of chopping alone. He had thought of everything possible to move the tree out of the way, chopping, pushing, pullies, and animals, but everything he tried had no effect.

Haran got to thinking of the purpose of this seemingly impossible task and then he got it. Orion had only said to have the trail clear before the sun set, he had never said to move the tree out of the way. So, Haran climbed to the top of the fallen tree seeing where the trail was on the other side, and he began to work, setting his marks and cutting two lines about a meter wide, just enough space for a horse to walk through. He chopped and chopped for what felt like all day, but truthfully it was only a few hours. He walked into the clearing at around two where he saw Orion training with Lyra on hand-to-hand combat; Haran walked up to the sand pit and watched them carefully. Orion threw multiple jabs to Lyra's body; she dropped her guard to defend it. To counter, Lyra threw a left hook, Orion ducked under the blow. Without skipping a beat in his fight said, "Nice of you to join us Haran, did you clear the trail or have yah given up already." He finished as he swept her leg and put her in the sand, finishing the spar.

"I finished your task, is there any other pointless task that I should do before I can start the actual training?" Haran asked, a little fed up with his so called "training."

Lyra, knowing what was about to happen, spoke before Orion, "Listen Haran, I was in your position only two months ago I know it seems pointless, but trust me it all serves a purpose."

Orion sighed, he had fun tormenting the boy, but he needed to get him started. "Tomorrow, tomorrow is when you I will explain everything, but your done for today, you as well Lyra I have to deal with a problem with a farmer's animals being killed," Orion said as he turned around to saddle up his horse, but he turned back to say one last thing, "Oh, and Haran, adequate work today boy, there might be hope for you yet."

As his urged his horse through the cut tree he was really impressed by the boy's problem-solving skills, he would never say that of course, because he would not want to get Haran overconfident because an unwarranted ego is something no teacher wants their pupils to have.

"Do you want to go for a walk," asked Lyra to Haran as they had nothing to do and were bored.

Haran responded with a "Sure, should we take the animals you think?"

"Of course, I never go anywhere without Scarlett," she said as she watched Haran put the baby lion in his satchel.

As they made their way out of the woods through an exit opposite of the one Orion left through. Haran asked "So, you've been with Orion for two months huh, if you don't mind me asking where you were before."

Lyra replied sadly, "Well I am originally from Dalhurst, but my parents died in a Bianet raid four months ago and I lived with my aunt and uncle on a farm near Calcore Canyon until Orion just appeared one day and recruited me to be a part of the Outryders, and now I am here with you."

"Well, I am sorry about your parents, but at least Orion saw something in you," Haran said sympathetically. By this time, they had made it to a small clearing through the woods.

"Well, what about you stranger, what's your sob story" she said jokingly, and Haran told her everything from how he was left on the Baron's front door, to the day he was recruited.

"I really do not know how Orion chooses his Recons, it seems so random, but what about your little friend? what is its name?" Lyra asked as she let Scarlett run out into the small clearing. Haran let the lion out of his satchel, who went to join Scarlett in her adventures.

"It's a her and honestly I don't really know, but I was thinking about calling her Spots," Haran replied, frowning as he heard Lyra laughing at his suggestion.

"You are not calling that cute little thing Spots over my dead. How about Shiva, god of life and compassion in the Athon religion," Lyra said, seemingly knowing a lot about the Athon culture. As much as Haran wanted to not like her suggestion he could not, it just fit so perfectly.

"Yeah, Shiva, you know you got a real knack for this stuff, first Scarlett and now Shiva," said Haran. "How'd you find Scarlett anyway," he asked her as he saw the two animals fighting playfully.

"I found her a few months ago, right before I first started with Orion. I was at Calcore exploring the caves when I saw her being chased by wolves. She climbed so high that the wolves couldn't get her, but they waited at the bottom until she had to come down. So I chased off the wolves and took her home with me." Lyra said recounting the events.

By the time they got back to the cabin it was dusk, and as soon as Haran hit his bed he passed out from exhaustion. Orion woke him early the next morning and took him back around the house to the training area. Lyra was already out there playing with Scarlett, "The Outryders are a group of fearless, calculated, and effective fighting force who have 70 fully trained members, one for every fief, and thirty-five more members over the world," he said as he dropped a cloth wrapped bundle to the ground in front of Haran. "And these are the basics of what we use," Orion continued, as he unrolled the cloth to reveal two short, one-handed axes, there was also a sash which had what looked like two dozen throwing knives, and of course, the Outryder cloak.

"These are the staples of all Outryders equipment. First, the axes, these are obviously wooden, seeing as the metal used to make our axes is extremely rare and your two are being forged as we speak, but they weigh the same, so they are effective for practice. These axes come from the Bianet raiders and are highly effective for close combat, they make little noise when you move, and they are not long and clunky like swords." Orion continued looking at Haran's face for recognition. After Haran nodded his acknowledgement, he continued, "The throwing knives are specially balanced for speed and deadliness; A well trained Outryder can throw these things with accuracy from a hundred meters away," Orion demonstrated in a swift movement striking a target thirty meters away in the center of the target Haran flinched, holding his chest.

"Finally, the cloak, this is what you use after you start throwing or the axes if you learn to use this effectively and you will never have to fight. The first principle of the Outryders is to stay silent and the second is to be efficient. Before we get to that, why don't you just practice throwing the knives and after a couple hours, I will teach you the way of the axe." Orion gesturing pointing to the target ten meters away and he began moving to the sand pit where Lyra was training.

It took Haran twenty times to even hit the target, and when he did it was in the leg. He started hitting it more consistently after about an hour of practicing. Two hours later Orion called Haran over by this time he could hit the target seventy percent of the time.

Orion called Haran over to the sand pit, "Ok Haran I will teach you the basic techniques of axe fighting now. For now, we will start with the one and eventually move to two," Orion said handing him an axe, and Haran nodded, "Get in a basic fighting position," Orion continued. Haran had been in his fair share of fights with Lottie, so he got into the fighting position he thought was correct. Orion knocked his front foot forward an inch and continued, "So first you will learn how to block every cut because if you have no defense there is no need for offense."

"Why is that?" Haran interrupted.

Orion responded with a simple, "Because if you have no defense you will be dead before you can even attack." Haran nodded, and Orion continued, "So pick up you weapon and show me what you got." Haran picked up the axe and Orion swung three slow cuts: side cut, diagonal cut, vertical cut. Haran struggled a little, but he blocked every cut, so Orion threw them again, but a little faster this time, side-diagonal-vertical.

After ten minutes, Orion threw new cuts the opposite way, eventually after he had shown every cut Orion swung faster, each cut bouncing off the next, side-diagonal-vertical-side-vertical-diagonal-vertical. It seemed there was no pattern to his cuts, but he each one bounced off the other in a show of grace and mastery. Ten seconds after he kicked it up Haran could not handle it, but as soon as Orion had about hit him with the sharpened side of the axe, he switched it the blunt side giving Haran a bruised rib and a hurt ego.

Haran collapsed clutching his side, "ouch," he said a little annoyed.

Overhead, Orion saw a pigeon fly to a tree ten meters away, this tree is where the pigeon was trained to go to when released from wherever the message was coming from; he went over to tree and read the message. He called Lyra over and she came, "Practice with Haran, I have to go deal with something at the Battleschool," Lyra nodded, and they started. Orion saddle up his horse and left the clearing thirty seconds later.

After an hour more of practicing blocking Haran got tired, so he went to do some more knife throwing. Thunk… Thunk, into the arm and leg of the wooden dummy, he still had to practice, but Haran was seeing massive improvement after a couple more hours.

Orion's horse came through the woods entrance around dusk, Haran noticed the entrance and approached Orion, "What happened at the Battleschool," Haran asked.

"Nothing, just a stupid fight over some kid messing up the training exercise they were doing this morning," Orion said with a tone that sounded as he was fed up.

"Do you know who," Haran asked trying not to sound nosey.

"No idea I just threw one of them in the river and went on to deal with more important things." Orion said finishing the conversation.

Somehow knowing Lottie was involved, Haran was worried because three years ago Haran and Lottie were best friends, until one day they went exploring Calcore Canyon. It was a late summer day that Haran remember very vividly. They were walking down the natural walkway down the canyon, Lottie got too close to the edge and it crumbled below his feet leaving him falling 150 feet below him. Luckily for Lottie there was a small tree branch sticking out from the sheer face of the canyon walls, so he caught on to it with one of his hands. As he hung over the drop over the canyon he begged and pleaded for Haran to help him. Haran grabbed on Lottie's free arm and tried to pull Lottie up to no avail, he was too weak, and it would cost Lottie his life. After trying to lift him for a minute more, Haran told Lottie to hang on while he got his rope out to pull him up that way, but it was too late Lottie's hands were already slipping and in a matter of seconds he would be dead.

As his best friend's hand slowly slid off the branch, Haran had screamed at the top of his lungs. He looked down to see his best friend desperately trying to grab onto something as he was dragged to his premature grave by gravity. After Lottie slid down the rock face fifteen meters or so, he barley grabbed a small outcropping rock down the face of the canyon and held onto it. However, in doing so he had gotten two long, deep gashes from his wrist to his elbow. Blood gushing from Lottie's arm, he looked around for anything to help him. That is when he saw a ledge just big enough for him to stand on only two meters away, and he swung himself onto it. Haran ran to go get a farmer not far from the canyon to tell him what happened. The farmer saved Lottie and bandaged up his wounds, but the real damage was done. Lottie would never forgive Haran for being so weak, and more importantly Haran would never forgive himself.

Chapter 6

❁

Lottie was approached by Battlemaster Gilpin shortly after dinner on the night of the tests. The day after Lottie had been asked to be a part of the Battleschool by Battlemaster Gilpin he went to the Battleschool and started his first day. The Battleschool is separated into four groups, first year, second year, third year, and fourth year. Lottie was obviously in the first year, so he started his day with The Rocks, which is holding a giant stone above your head for at least ten minutes and if one person drops their stone the whole thing restarts. After he did The Rocks, he had Tactics 1 taught by a Sir Lerin, Sir Lerin was an old retired strategist for the royal army, after he lost his leg in a fire, he decided he was going to teach the younger generations. It was a valiant cause, even if he was harsh in teaching style.

After the two hours of boring class, Lottie got up to leave for breakfast, that's when he noticed a slightly built individual who looked as if they had a weird looking head covering walking out of the class. The head covering was a purple fabric that covered the boy's entire hair and ears. He looked on, very confused at why anyone would want to wear that thing.

An hour after breakfast Lottie had his first collective training session where Battlemaster Gilpin put the first years in a basic tournament to see where everyone was at. The first round was between two boys that Lottie didn't know, one named Grew and the other named Francis. Grew looked as if he had never carried a sword before in his life, whereas Francis, the blacksmith's son, had his fair share of knowledge of a sword. They performed mediocre 'strokes' in which Francis was getting the upper hand until finally Grew slipped on the sand in a pathetic attempt at a thrust. The first fight went to Francis; many other fights went the same way or even worse. Until it came to the boy with the cover's turn, the boy was named El apparently, and he was very efficient with the sword. He both timed his shots and delivered them in a way that sent his opponent sprawling on the ground in a matter of seconds. As Lottie saw the boy's performance, he thought he might actually have some competition. Lottie spent most of his time at the castle with a sword in hand, so he easily dispatched his opponent in three strokes. One more hour of the worst sword fighting ever, and it was Lottie's turn against the boy with the covering. On Gilpin's orders, they circled each other with their wooden swords that were just sticks with a cross-guard. El was the first to strike, an overhead cut came straight down on Lottie's head; Lottie parried the strike and responded with a side cut. El danced back gracefully to avoid the cut and threw an underhand cut to Lottie's left leg. Lottie, seemingly effortlessly, jumped over the cut and they reset. Gilpin, seeing how long it would take for the fight to end, decided to end it prematurely, "Alright, that's enough," he said loudly.

"But Battlemaster, we have only just begun," Lottie protested, and his demeanor changed from one of excitement for a new challenge to one of disappointment.

"Lottie, there is an old Ushayian proverb that goes something like this, 'there is no victory in prolonged warfare'. If I let you fight all day then you don't get to go to lunch early, that being said," he stopped looked to all the first years, "Everyone go to lunch."

At lunch Lottie saw the figure with the weird head covering, El, again at a table in the back, so he sat down next to him. "Hey, you are pretty good, " Lottie said genuinely.

A higher pitched voice came back almost like a girl, "Thanks."

Lottie nodded and asked another question "Your slim, but surprisingly good, how'd you end up here anyway?"

The voice came back, "I saved the Battlemaster's life, so he offered a spot in the Battleschool for me."

Lottie responded by nodding his head then offering a handshake, "Names Lottie, and I am looking to finish our fight"

"Any time, any place, I'm ready," El responded.

"Well, El do you have History of Anjagor 1 next," Lottie asked.

"Yes," El responded.

"Ok then I will see you there," Lottie said getting up and as he was walking to his next class he thought, there was something strange about that boy.

History was boring as ever; Sir Fredrick taught about how the nation was formed for two hours. Sir Fredrick along with Sir Lerin were directly under Battlemaster Gilpin and together they taught the classes while the Battlemaster, along with some fourth-year students taught the basic fighting. After history was the last and most dreadful exercise of the day, The Run. The Run was a five-kilometer run going through the tall grass of Malen Plains with a bag full of rocks on your back to touch the castle and back.

There were fourth years running alongside you every step of the way. Of course they didn't have a bag full of rocks to carry, so it was way easier for them. If you walked for even a second, they took dinner away from you, and the only thing worse than all these grueling exercises was going to bed hungry. Lottie made it halfway before he stopped, even if he got the furthest without stopping, he still failed. By the time Lottie got back he went straight to bed, within twenty minutes everyone else was inside, and Lottie was asleep. The next couple days were about the same as the first, but Lottie got to know El a little bit more. He found out that El was originally from Osmole, a relatively wealthy fief which laid due east of Norhall. Osmole was a mining fief based off the fact that it, along with other fiefs lined the Chien Mountains to the east.

As Lottie had finished his Tactics class, he was getting ready for Gilpin's training. However, he forgot his practice sword in the dorm room; as he walked into the dorm rooms, he saw the most beautiful girl he had ever seen at El's bunk. Her golden hair flowing as if it were the ocean waves cresting and troughing along her back, and her eyes looked as of they were made from jade. Now that he thought about it, El's eyes were that color.

"El?" he asked," Is that you," she reached for her head covering sitting on the bed, but before she could get it Lottie grabbed her hand saying, "Hey, its ok, you can trust me with your secret...."

El interrupted just a little annoyed someone had found out her secret so fast, "We can't talk now," she said. "But I'll explain everything after training, trust me."

Today, Gilpin did simple basic strokes training because after what he saw during their tournament, it looked like they needed it. He would call out basic strokes like side cut, thrust, overhand, and underhand, and they were to launch a combo in unison before they went to lunch. Suffice it to say they went to lunch late; at lunch, El explained herself. El's name was Ella Frenger and she had saved Battlemaster Gilpin on her way to her mother's place near Norhall. She was rather good with a sword already because her grandfather was the Battlemaster for the Osmole fief, so when a group of half a dozen bandits on the road attacked Gilpin while she was on the way to her mother, she dispatched two of them with ease while Gilpin handled the other four. Gilpin thanked her and offered her a place at the Battleschool. However, since she was a girl, Gilpin gave her the head covering to keep on her head at all time. "If those boys know you are a girl, I'm afraid you might have more than a sword in you if you go," he said as when he offered her the spot. As she finished her story, Lottie was shocked as she told him the part about her parents being near Norhall, he had been here since he was little and had not seen anyone resembling Ella ever, so he promptly asked, "What does she do?"

"I don't really know, what she does, all my grandpa said was that she told him on my sixteenth birthday to send me to find her," Ella said.

"And what of your dad?" Lottie asked already knowing the answer when he saw her face shift.

Ella responded with a shuddering breath, "My dad was murdered right in front of my eyes by the Athons, and I was glad to see them pack up and go home after the Norhall fief and the legendary Orion utterly defeated them at The Battle of The Anvil." Lottie nodded in response not knowing how to respond, and as the bell sounded to go to his History of Anjagor class with a newfound respect for the pretty girl under the head covering.

Lottie was the only one to make it back from The Run, it was his first time in the three days he has been here and he got a hefty serving hot soup and soft bread, as payment. When everyone got back, he was already soaking his bread in his second bowl of soup. Gilpin was surprised to see the natural athleticism and fighting ability of Lottie, for he had already mastered the basic strokes and was already adding new strokes that switched up the pattern of strokes that Gilpin had called out. The Battlemaster knew he would have to start training with Lottie personally tomorrow, trying to think of a way to tell him without getting him too cocky. He eventually approached him before everyone went to bed telling Lottie that there was potential in him to be a great warrior.

The next morning during the Stones, an annoying kid named Grew kept dropping his stone making everyone restart. This happened five time, five times holding a heavy stone above their heads for ten minutes each time, by about the fourth time Lottie got angry at the kid. By the fifth time Lottie was furious, and at breakfast he approached Grew angry at his weakness. "What is your problem Grew can you not lift a stupid little rock," he said aggressively.

"I'm sorry Lottie, I just couldn't do it today I was sore from yesterday," Grew said defensively. Lottie had dealt with weakness his whole life, his parents abandoned him, his best friend gave him scars, and now this, he was so sick and tired of weakness. He looked at the scars down his arm and he looked up at Grew. He grabbed him by the collar of his shirt, and he drew his fist back, but just before he snapped, Grew's friend Terence tackled him to the ground and started wailing on him.

Lottie pushed Terence off of him and when got up to fight back, he looked around to see everyone else in the cafeteria fighting. So he decided to get in on it; displaying his power his dispatched two with a short flurry of punches, he looked around reveling at the circumstance he had found himself in.

Battlemaster Gilpin stopped it all in a matter of seconds, "STOP FIGHTING," he bellowed, and everyone stopped, "Who started it? WHO STARTED IT?" every eye turned to Lottie and Grew. They were dragged to the Battlemaster's office, where they waited, and waited, and waited for the Battlemaster, or someone to return. The awkward silence filling the room, but neither boy spoke. Finally, after hours of waiting the Battlemaster showed up with Orion and his dreadful appearance.

Before anyone even spoke, Orion just grabbed Lottie by the collar with his iron grip and just walked him to his horse.

"Get on," he said and Lottie obeyed unquestioningly. For a kilometer they rode in silence. They reached the edge of the Wolf's Tail, "Get off," Orion said. When Lottie got off, Orion simply grabbed him by the collar and threw him into the frigid water of the Wolf's Tail. When Lottie came up and got out of the water he said, "That bastard Orion, he'll pay for this". Lottie got back to the Battle school twenty minutes later soaking wet and miserable, but he still had to go to personal training with Battlemaster Gilpin. Who had told him the day before to meet him in the training arena when the others were doing The Run.

Personal training with Gilpin took place of The Run for Lottie's end of day activities. Lottie met Gilpin in the arena outside the dorms, however there were far less people so Gilpin could train Lottie one on one. "First what you are going to do is choose your weapon or weapons," The Battlemaster said pointing to rack against the wall of weapons; it contained all sorts of weapons including, sword, axes, spears and halberds. Lottie studied the weapons, they all looked so appealing, but he already knew his choice "I want to duel wield swords," he had learned about the different weapons and their uses in his Tactics class.

"Ok, pick them up and let's get started," Gilpin responded acknowledging the deadliness of the simple combination, he himself had used them when he was fighting in the war against the Frelorians, but soon after he realized they were not the best for defense. So he started diversifying his weapon choice to become a master of all of them. They started slow, the strokes obviously indicated seconds before they hit their intended target, after half an hour or so, they picked up the pace each blow striking off the next in a brilliant flash of swordsmanship from both parties. However, Gilpin had been using his weapons, the sword and shield, for longer and he was a very experience fighter, so he very clearly got the upper hand in the engagement.

After about half an hour more of this, they stopped, "Great work today Lottie," the Battlemaster said admirably.

"Thank you, sir, and I just have to ask, is there any tricks you know about keeping calm during an actual engagement," Lottie asked, thinking how he would react if his life were actually in danger. The Battlemaster knew exactly what he meant, in battle, many nonexperience soldiers will go red with rage and start killing everyone.

"Meet me at Calcore Canyon at midnight tomorrow, I will show you exactly what you have to do," the Battlemaster responded with a hint of a grin on his face.

Lottie showed up to the bottom of the rocky canyon that was Calcore where he saw Gilpin already waiting for him outside a small cave. A pack of hungry wolves stood before him, snarling and howling wildly, Lottie tried to run over to help him, but Gilpin signaled for him to stop. As the wolves drew in closer that is when he saw it, the fear in the wolves' eyes and the absence of fear in Battlemaster Gilpin's.

"You see Lottie, you cannot be afraid of anything when in a fight for your life, you need laser focus and you also need to know your opponent. Their next five moves and how to counter them; for you to truly be a master, you first need to master your brain, and to do that you have to master your emotions." Gilpin finished, and seeing that their opponent was not scared or not threating them, they went back to their cave where they kept watchful eyes. Lottie smiled to himself, this was going to be fun.

Chapter 7

It was the next night before Lottie really got started with mastering his pent-up emotions, and it was unlike anything he had ever experienced. Again, Gilpin was waiting on him at the bottom of Calcore, however this time there were no wolves growling at him. They just simple sat calmly in their cave, watching the human to see what he was doing. When he got there, Gilpin had drawn out a small circle only about three meters in diameter around himself. Lottie had been told to not bring his swords for this part, so he didn't. Lottie walked up to Gilpin and pointed to the makeshift circle, "What's this for, I thought we were mastering my emotions."

Not even acknowledging the question Gilpin just simply replied with, " Lottie, there is an old quote that goes like this, 'A man with a lack of balance in his life is far less dangerous than that of a man who is perfectly balanced.' You see my boy, life itself is balance, there is no light without darkness, no joy without misery, no hope without despair. Every thing has its own balance. But what is the opposite of anger?"

Lottie though for a moment, but nothing came to mind, "No idea."

Gilpin smiled, "The opposite of anger is fear, there is not one without the other. Now, people who start fights are either afraid, or angry, and I know you are not afraid, so why are you angry son."

Lottie thought back to all the times he has been let down in his life, "I am angry because my father abandoned me, my best friend gave me scars and my mother didn't think me good enough to live around for. I am angry because I have been let down my whole ENTIRE LIFE with NO ONE BY MY SIDE." Lottie, after recalling all the terrible things that had happened in his life, began to cry.

"And you are AFRAID, that if you let anyone in to your life, they will just disappoint you again," Gilpin said trying to prove his point.

Lottie looked up, tears streaming down his face, "Yes, I am afraid that if I am let down again, I might snap."

"There is nothing wrong with fear and anger Lottie, in fact they are the most powerful of emotions, we just need to learn how to harness them," Gilpin said as he saw the tears start to dry. "Now, lets get started. Who are you most angry with in your life?"

It was a hard decision, his father had abandoned him, scaring him, but Haran had given him scars, "Haran." He said finally, surprised at his own answer.

"Ahh, the other orphan boy. Well, I bet you didn't know he was an Outryder now did you," Gilpin asked.

"Wait, Haran is an Outryder," Lottie asked shocked at how Haran could possibly be an Outryder.

"Oh yes, and Orion will train him to be a machine, so why don't you pretend I am him and strike me," Gilpin said trying to goad Lottie to hit him.

"I will not attack my master," Lottie said offended that Gilpin asked him to do so.

"I am not your master, I am Haran, now STRIKE ME," Gilpin screamed the last part which set Lottie into action. A big right hand came from the large boy, straight to the Battlemaster's face. Gilpin slipped just to the right of the punch, coming under the strike and delivered a startling blow to Lottie's exposed kidneys. Lottie backed up and started wheezing uncontrollably, by the time that he finished he managed to croak out a sentence, "What was that for?"

"It might have been easy to take your anger out on Haran in the past, but it won't be so easy next time, he's a Outryder now, and he will know how to defend himself. And even if you might be good with a sword, you are a crappy fighter." Gilpin said to the boy. Lottie was offended, but there was truth in the statement, he never really was the best fighter, he was just simply bigger than Haran and that won him most every fight. However, next time, Haran will be trained, and he will want revenge from all the times Lottie bullied him. "Again," Gilpin said as he got into a fighting position in the center of the circle. Lottie did the same thing, came over the top with a wild right hand and Gilpin shifted his weight back, just enough to avoid the shot, and planted his right hand in Lottie's exposed face. Not hard enough to seriously hurt him, but hard enough to get his point across. "Again," he said as Lottie got back up. Lottie did so, but was a little more tentative this time, there was no reason for him to be hurting himself like this. He circled his master, watching his every step very visibly under the stars. This time, instead of going straight for the wild right hand, he faked that he was, in which Gilpin leaned back and Lottie threw a jab to his face. Gilpin, not expecting it, barely got his head out of the way only to sweep Lottie and leave him sprawling on the ground. "Better, again." They continued like this long into the night, each time Lottie getting a little better. Until they finally decided it was best to get some rest before the next morning.

The next day Lottie did the same thing he did every day, Rocks, class, breakfast, group training with Gilpin, etc. He walked out to do his personal training with Gilpin, and hope he wouldn't have to fight his master today. Luckily, Gilpin had the wooden dummies up, presumably to teach him more combos. Gilpin was already warming up, so Lottie walked over to him, "Hey I have been meaning to ask you, did you know my father at all."

"Sadly no Lottie, he left the year before I started as Battlemaster, but I am sure he left for a good reason," Gilpin said to Lottie, truthfully, he hadn't seen anyone with Lottie's natural skill ever. His father must have surely been a force to be reckoned with if Lottie were any example. Lottie silently cursed, he had hoped that Gilpin could tell him something about his father. After they warmed up, Gilpin started him on a complex combination of cuts and slashes all performed excellently multiple times. After he saw that Lottie had learned all the strokes, Gilpin looked over and saw a fourth-year boy posting something on the wall to the dorm rooms. "HEY" he yelled from across the training fields. "You are supposed to be on the Run," Gilpin said as he went to go investigate what the boy was doing. Lottie stopped his strokes after he heard Gilpin yell, and followed behind him. Gilpin stopped just before reaching the boy, "What are you doing son," Gilpin said loudly.

"Sorry Battlemaster, I didn't mean to interrupt your training, but we just got these new flyers in and Sir Lerin told me to put them up." The boy said a little frighted, he knew how vicious the Battlemaster could be at times.

"Ok, just post them and get out of here, I will talk to Lerin later. What are they anyway?" Gilpin said as he pushed through the boy to see the posters. It was a large poster with a sword and shield crossed on the front. On the top it read in bold letters, " **Young Men to the Call: Fighting tournament at Norhall on the first of September,**". Gilpin looked visibly shocked, everything that had to deal with combats and Norhall went by him, so why hadn't he heard of this until now. He made a mental note to talk to Baron Ligate about this in the morning. The fourth year looked at him skeptically, wondering what he should do next. "Go ahead," Gilpin said, as he looked at the boy.

Gilpin turned around, and walked back to the training area, Lottie followed. "Why would you let him keep them up?" Lottie asked curiously. Gilpin looked at Lottie and said, "You have just over a month." Lottie was confused by what he meant, so he said, "A month for what?"

"To train for that tournament, so let's get going," Gilpin said as he started drawing out another circle in the sand of the training area. Lottie looked and whispered quietly to himself. "Alright, let's go.

Chapter 8

Gilpin knocked on the Baron's office about an hour after dawn, he knew Ligate would be awake, Ligate woke up at dawn each day and went straight into his office to get an early start. "Come in," he heard the Baron call from the other side of the door. Gilpin pushed the door open and walked in to the office, "Well hey Battlemaster what can I do for you," Ligate said tiredly.

"I was just wondering about this tournament that I have been hearing about. Why hadn't it come to my attention until now," Gilpin said a little aggressively.

"Ah yes that," Ligate said as he stood up from his desk. "Orion approached me the other day and suggested a tournament for the boys of Norhall to compete in. He thought it would be good for his new apprentice and the boys of the Battleschool to compete to gain experience in hand-to hand-combat. And I think it is a splendid idea, obviously there will be rules so no one would get hurt. And he even offered a very substantial reward for the winner, 500 silvers."

Gilpin was awestruck, that was a lot of money, especially for a child, "FIVE HUNDRED SILVERS for a child is he insane or just stupid?"

Ligate just laughed, " I'd like to think we are all a little insane at times. However, it is a substantial amount so we should get boys from all over Norhall. And if you find some good enough, you can recruit them." Gilpin knew the Baron was right, but he was still a little angry that it had not gone through him first and just finished the conversation, "Alright, deal."

Lyra, Haran and Orion were all sitting at the table eating breakfast, "What do you mean I cant fight in the tournament?" Lyra said to Orion furiously. She was a far better fighter than Haran at this point.

"Listen Lyra, I realize you are upset, but they will not let girls fight. It's a politics thing, obviously I know you can run circles on those boys, but the people of Anjagor wont allow it." Orion said trying to reassure Lyra. It worked slightly, but she was still angry with the stupid law.

"It doesn't matter anyway, if you were to get to the final round you would lose to me anyway," Haran knew it wasn't true, at least not yet, but if he kept up the hard work he could beat her one day.

"Oh yeah, well let's go right now weasel boy," Lyra said as she lunged across the table at Haran. Haran practically jumped out of his seat, and made a mental note to stop talking to Lyra when she is angry.

"That being said, Lyra, you will have to train with Haran a little more on his hand-to-hand combat in the next month so he can be prepared for the boys at the Battleschool. Those boys will be the ones you have to look out for." He said addressing Haran who nodded his acknowledgement. He wondered if Lottie was going to be there, if he was, he would surly have to face him eventually, and that alone scared Haran. Lyra shook her head yes, even though he really wanted to fight by herself. The least she could do was help Haran win.

Orion was the first to walk out to help train Haran, they walked up to the sand pit used for training Orion stopped in the middle. "Alright, so first let's teach you how to throw the basic punches," Orion said. Haran followed Orion's lead and stood just with his feet just over shoulder width apart with his right foot back. "Alright, looking good, now, on your toes," Orion said showing him what to do.

47

Haran did as he said, "Good, now, this is a jab," Orion threw his front fist out stepping about an inch forward with his left foot. "A jab is used to keep you opponent at distance if you are larger, but you will be using it as a distraction for your right hand," Orion jabbed, but as his hand was coming back, his right hand shot forward with blistering speed, hips twisted, foot planted firmly on the ground, and head low. After Orion showed Haran the cross, he showed him a hook then an uppercut.

They had been out there for about an hour when Orion said, "Alright, show me what you got."

Orion had expected Haran to pick this up just as fast as he had with his axes, but it didn't seem he would be that lucky. Haran tentatively approached Orion, slowly sliding his feet through the sand; Orion simply stood still in the center waiting for his opponent to strike. When he finally did, it was a half-hearted jab followed by what some would call a hook, but it looked more like a child's slap then anything. "Seriously Haran, you are going to have to be better than this if you're going to stand a chance."

Haran shook his head defiantly, he was scared, he knew that if he actually trained he could make it to the final round, but that also meant he would have to face Lottie. Orion stopped, and looked on amazed for the first time in a very long time. Haran was the ideal pupil, he was athletic, ingenious, and above all, he was a hard worker. However, this Haran was different, he was a scared little kitten in front of a howling wolf, and that fear alone scared Orion. "What's wrong Haran? This isn't you," Orion said as he threw down his practice axes.

"Orion," Haran said as he stood still head hung low with is hood cast over his head. "I'm scared, scared that I will lose to the boy I can't let win."

Orion now understood his new Recon's feelings, torn between pride and a feeling of duty, "Listen Haran." Haran looked up slightly meeting his master's eyes, "If you let fear dictate what could happen in life, nothing will happen at all. If you lose before you face this boy, you will regret that you didn't have the guts to face him. But if you face him with guts and courage, you will earn his respect, win or lose."

Haran knew Orion was right, and he also knew that he would have to train hard if he were to beat Lottie. "Alright," he said finally, "Let's go."

Chapter 9

The month flew by as if it were days, between his regular training and his fighting training. However, even though time flew by, Haran felt that he was improving every day. He noticed he was sharper and more calculated, and instead of just punching arbitrarily; he planned every punch to set up the next as if it were an active chess game in seconds of time. Not to say he was on the likes of Orion, but he showed competition for Lyra. The tournament was set for the first of September, tomorrow. Haran sat up from his bed next to the window, the night sky casting down on him with the weight of hours of training. Even though Haran felt as if he were well prepared, he didn't feel ready. He got out of bed and tiptoed carefully into the main room, Shiva popped her head up. "Come," Haran whispered as the perfectly oiled hinged creeped open. Shiva followed her master into the surprisingly well lit night. As Haran got outside, there was a slight breeze that came over him. He walked further into the yard looking at the stars above him. A beautiful cluster appeared above his head, one that looked like a hunter looking for his next prey. After a few moments, he looked back to see Shiva looking up to him curiously. "What do I do Shiva, if I lose Lottie will never let it down, but if I win, I fear I will lose myself in the process." Haran asked actually expecting an answer for a moment. Then he realized he was talking to a cat and he headed off to bed.

The tournament, held just outside the Battleschool, was a very lively affair with people from all over Norhall. Stalls of venders were wrapped around the fighting arenas; there were about ten arenas in total, all with perfectly cut grass and level ground. There were about 150 boys ranging drastically in size waiting to be assigned a number. This number would decide who they would go against in the first match, randomly selected from a shuffled box of papers. After waiting in the line for a few minutes, it was Haran's turn, after pulling out the paper he read it, his number was 5.

After everyone finished picking out their number, everyone waited to hear the rules of the tournament. Baron Ligate got up on a slightly raised platform and began to speak. "Young men of Norhall, today you will be fiercely competing against your peers in hand-to-hand combat. However, as a safety precaution, we will have to ask you to wear these padded gloves," Ligate held up gloves with an inch or so of padding, it would soften the blow, but not by much. "Also you will only be able to throw punches, if you do not wish to follow by these rules you will be disqualified." He stepped down eager to see the fights that were about to unfold from Norhall's finest. Barte, Ligate's assistant, was the one who made the brackets for the tournament. The brackets went like this, since there were exactly one-hundred and fifty people there, everyone will fight in the first round against the number next to them: one would fight two, three would fight four, five would fight six, etc. The second round there would only have 75 people left so the five highest performers would get a by to the third round. The third will only have 35 people plus the five who got the by which made 40 people in total. The rounds would continue forward until it was down to ten where Barte would have to make a new bracket.

Haran, being number five, was one of the first people to fight. After getting his gloves on, he stepped up to the arena, his opponent was already across from him. His opponent, one of Udo's apprentices named Ferric, stood across the arena from him; he was slightly bigger than Haran with a very defined upper body from the constant banging of the Norhall forge. Laser-focused with Orion behind him as his master and trainer, Haran could not lose until he faced Lottie, he would not lose. A giant bell rung through the air, the signal to start, Haran circled his opponent moving clock-wise. He immediately noticed that his opponent was left-handed, an unorthodox opponent to face seeing as many people in Anjagor were right-handed. They circled each other, each waiting for the other to make the first move. After a few more seconds, Ferric grew impatient and threw a jab into Haran's guard. Haran took the punch without flinching and threw a deadly left hook to counter. Ferric's knees buckled under the blow, but he still stood after, which alone was respectable. The crowd, who were observing other fights happening at the time, suddenly turned their heads towards Haran. Ferric, still stunned from the hit, tried to throw a jab then a cross, but it simply bounced off Haran's guard weakly. Haran, feeling bad for the poor, unprepared boy, threw a light cross to Ferric's body, sending him crumbling to the floor. Oohs and aahs came from the crown as Haran finished the fight. The eyes were on him, and that what gave him the by for the second round.

Lottie had chosen number 109, so he was one of the last fighters to fight in the first round. He hadn't seen Haran's fight, but he heard the word that Haran dispatched his opponent in two punches. Lottie expected as much from the Recon, but he hadn't expected the recognition Haran would receive from just one fight. Lottie pushed thoughts of Haran out of his mind, he had to focus on the task at hand for now. He stepped into the arena and got the first glimpse at his opponent, Grew. He had wanted his revenge on Grew and his friend for the lunch fight since it happened, and now was the perfect opportunity. He smiled to himself as the bell sounded out the start and began to press forward with his hands dropped below his waist. He didn't need to guard against the likes of Grew, in fact Grew never even threw a punch. Lottie advanced so fast that Grew didn't know what to do, and before he could do anything, Lottie delivered a beautifully executed uppercut directly under Grew's chin. Grew was lifted inches into the air and plummeted to the ground, out cold. The crowd took at second to realize the fight was over, but when they did they were silent; that was the most vicious knockout they had ever seen. Lottie had earned his spot for the by round, like it or not.

Chapter 10

The third and fourth rounds for the two boys were much like the first; Haran would counter a missed strike from his opponent, and Lottie would brute force his way through. However, in the fifth round, the round with the top ten, the boys were actually challenged. Haran went up against a fourth year from the Battleschool, Aiden. Aiden was big, like many in the Battleschool, and surprisingly fast for his size. But, after five minutes of wearing down from Haran, Aiden crumbled. Lottie struggled just as much against his opponent; a boy named Crainer. He wasn't as big as Lottie, but not by much, and what he lacked in size, he made up for in speed and precision. Lottie started off like he had the other times, bolting in with a jaw shattering punch hoping to send his opponent reeling. However, Crainer was better than the others Lottie faced, and ducked under the shot and threw a flurry of uppercuts to Lottie's body. Lottie hardly flinched, nothing would keep him from getting at Haran in the finals. He plowed forward taking shot after shot to the head and body, but he was unfazed, and that alone got in his opponent's head. After realizing that there was no way he could be the tank that was Lottie, Crainer slowed giving Lottie the opportunity to throw an unexpected cross which sent Crainer down. The next round there would be five contestants remaining, which meant someone got the by to the finals. That someone was Haran, after his performance against Aiden, it was an obvious choice.

The next round was the round before the semi-finals, Lottie had only two more opponents to go before he faced his old friend. His opponent for the semi-finals had already been decided before he fought, so he decided to show Haran what he was capable of. As he stood across the grass arena from his opponent who was already frightened at what Lottie would do to him he looked over to Barte, "You know what, let me fight both of them at once," Lottie said as he pointed to his opponent for the semi-finals.

"What? You want to fight two at once," Barte said shocked from the outrageous demand.

"Yes, I have run out of patience for this stupid tournament." Lottie said angry that he was this close to his goal.

"I suppose we could do that, if the contestants are ok with it," Barte said trying to entertain the crowd. The remaining fighters agreed seeing it as their only way to beat Lottie, and both fighters stepped into the ring.

"And one last thing, Haran," Lottie said locating Haran in the front of the crown.

"What Lottie," Haran said stone-faced and serious.

"Take notes because you're next," Lottie said as the bell rang. Both Lottie's opponents approached him cautiously, if they attacked at two different angles they could overwhelm Lottie. At least that's what they thought. They were wrong because as one of the boys went for a cross on Lottie, he ducked under it and delivered a rib-shattering hook sending the boy across the arena and out into the crowd. The last boy, distracted by what he just saw, was sent flying right beside Haran by a right hand from Lottie. Haran looked at the boy in horror as he saw the boy's face, his nose was broken and he was bleeding profusely. Haran looked up at Lottie who met Haran's eyes. And that is when Haran realized that he would be fighting for his life.

The final round was set to take place just before at sunset, and that time was now. They had a special arena for the final round, one on a raised platform so that the crowd could see everything. As Haran stepped up to the platform, he shook his nerves off and waited patiently for Lottie to step into the arena. After Lottie got into the arena, the boys never broke eye contact, each set of eyes equally determined to win. The bell rung, it was finally time, they both circled, knowing the cost of striking first. Even though he knew that striking first would get him hurt, Lottie grew impatient. He bolted in throwing a lightning fast right hook. Haran ducked under easily and hit Lottie in the ribs; Lottie felt it immediately, he really underestimated the Haran's new strength. Sensing the weakness, Haran thought he could end the fight early and began throwing more punches at Lottie. However that was a mistake, Lottie slipped Haran's cross, ducked under his hook and retaliated with an uppercut that connected squarely with Haran's jaw. Haran's teeth clattered, but other than that he held up. After this, there was an instant realization, they were of equal skill, and they would be trading punches until midnight if something didn't change and fast.

After another trade, Haran was starting to grow hot with anger, he thought he had trained enough to beat Lottie, but he was mistaken. They traded again, Haran landing a hook and Lottie a cross; Haran grew angrier. Haran rushed in, thinking this time he would surly finish his old friend off, but to no avail. Orion, who was watching from the sidelines saw what was happening, and he knew how the fight would end if Haran continued this tact. Haran rushed in again, this time however, only Lottie landed a punch. Haran's head flew back, and Lottie capitalized, punishing Haran for his foolishness. "Get your head straight Haran," Orion yelled from behind him. But it was too late, Haran was furious now, he charged in again throwing punches wildly. One of the punches landed on Lottie's temple, sending him backwards. Haran tried to press forward, but Lottie had already recovered and ducked out of the way. Haran threw what was his final punch of the day, a haymaker which Lottie ducked under, and with a light right hook, Haran's knees touched the ground. The rules were, that if any part of your body touches the ground, you lose. The fight was over, Haran had lost.

Haran walked into the cabin after his loss, his head was hung low with devastation, "I cant believe I lost to Lottie again," he said as Orion and Lyra followed him inside.

Orion looked at Haran as would a disappointed father, "Listen Haran, you did not lose to Lottie."

"Oh really, because it sure does feel like I lost," Haran said rubbing his bruises.

"No, you lost, but just not to Lottie," Orion said which confused Haran.

"Who did I lose to then?" Haran asked trying to see Orion's point.

"You lost to yourself Haran, you let your emotions get the better of you. You were the better fighter today, but Lottie was a better man, " Orion said. Haran realized that Orion was right, he was getting the better of Lottie until he let his anger take control of him. "You're right," Haran said as his chest deflated, "I could have beat Lottie, and next time I will learn to control myself."

"That's what I like to hear," Orion said, "Now, tomorrow, we get back to training. But for tonight, we rest."

Chapter 11

After a month or so back at training, a courier delivered Haran his real axes in. They were a beautiful piece of art, a smooth wooden handle of red oak attached to a magnificent looking head. The head of the axes were blueish and layered, as if the craftsmen were to draw lines down the metal with the darker metal.

"It's called Toscalt, it is the hardest metal in the world, and it is virtually unbreakable," Orion said as he handed the axes to Haran.

During the month after the fight, Haran had gotten particularly good with the practice axes, he was already able to keep up with Lyra, and beat her half the time. He had also gotten good with the throwing knives, able to throw them quickly and effectively from any angle, standing, jumping left, jumping right, and crouching up to 75 meters. His throwing abilities were still miles away from the level that Lyra was on let alone Orion, but as Orion always said, "Two of the most powerful warriors alive are patience and time."

Out in the yard, Haran was getting a feel for his new axes when Orion came back from checking the snares. Orion, after seeing Haran's rapid improvement since the fight with Lottie decided it was time for him to receive his cloak. "Come Haran, its time for you to learn to use your greatest weapon." Haran followed Orion, a little confused at the meaning of the statement, but he knew it was best not to ask a stupid question when he was about to find the answer out. Orion led him about one hundred meters into the woods, where he stopped and dropped Haran his cloak. Haran had not actually used his cloak yet, and he still thought it might have magical powers. After a couple seconds Orion asked, "Do you remember what I told you our principles were the first time I gave you your weapons?"

"I believe it was something along the lines of 'Our first principle as Outryders is to stay silent and the second is to be efficient,'" Haran said trying to remember the exact phrasing.

"Precisely, and your greatest asset to those two things is that cloak right there," Orion said pointing at the green and brown cloak at Haran's feet. Haran was skeptical, but he put the cloak on, "They call it camouflage, it helps you blend in with your surroundings, and if you are still enough, it will make you look invisible."

Haran nodded, of course, it all made sense to him now, the rumors about them being able to become invisible at will, and the fact that they were the most effective fighting force in the world. It was all due to their ability to move silently and remain unseen to the naked eye.

"I have seen you're ability to sneak around the castle, but let us see how you do in the woods," Orion said as he walked a little farther into the woods, then he back to the clearing that they just came from, "I am going to go down there and you are going to try and sneak past me, and every time I see you or hear you, you get an extra hour out here with me. However, if you do get away, I will let you go and teach you a new trick."

He had already failed five times before his first hour was up, he had tried everything he thought to, brush, trees, long grass, but every single time, his master sent a throwing knife a meter from where he stood indicating he was aware that Haran was there. Then Haran remembered, the cloak, the main thing he was supposed to be using to stay hidden he was wearing like a normal piece of clothing; so, he used it, looking for places where the cloak would blend in the most.

This time he got closer, much closer than he had ever been before, and the next time he got closer, and the next, closer, and closer, and closer. Until finally, Orion said, looking at the spot Haran was at three meters away, "You have done well today, just keep practicing and we will try again in two days or so."

"What about the extra hours, and me getting past you," Haran asked.

"Only two people in the entirety of the Outryders have ever gotten past me, at your skill level now, it is an impossible feat," Orion said blankly. Haran was a little offended, but he knew Orion was right, this was his first day doing it, obviously he would not be the greatest at the start.

The next day, he was out with his lion, Shiva, she was still small, but he knew how big she was going to get, he had to feed her milk, and scraps, seeing as she could not hunt for herself yet. Shiva and Scarlett had become close since Haran arrived; Shiva would just follow Scarlett all day on her adventures through the woods when Haran was practicing. Haran had also gotten close with Lyra, between training together and spending their free time together they had become close friends. Haran was practicing some moves with Lyra when he looked over to Orion who was saddling up his horse. Lyra had her own horse named, Ranger, and Orion had his horse named, Nova, but Haran had yet to get his horse. Both Ranger and Nova were incredible horses, even though their appearance seemed small and unkempt they were some of the fastest horses he had ever seen in his life. WACK, Haran fell to the ground, distracted by his thoughts, he had let his guard down for just a couple seconds, and Lyra had accidentally hit him in the ribs with her practice axe, "Haran, pay attention, or next time I will really hurt you," Lyra said as she helped him to his feet.

Orion saw what happened from a distance and was now approaching them, "Haran, pack a bag, we are going on a trip for a day or so, Lyra tell the Baron to talk to you if he has a problem."

Lyra nodded, she already knowing where they were going, but kind of sad because he had not invited her. It would be good to see old Rowan again, but she knew someone had to be in Norhall if something bad happened.

After Haran packed his bag, they began heading to Anjagor, the capital. After about three hours of traveling they made it to the edge of Norhall, and about a kilometer from the border Orion stopped. "Remember what I told you about paying attention to your surroundings," he whispered, indicating to either side of the woods.

Haran was confused until he looked around, that is when he saw them, a little over a half dozen figures in the tree line. They were obviously trying to ambush any wealthy looking traveler that came along the beaten path.

However, Haran and Orion were not any random traveler, Orion was an Outryder and even if Haran had only been a Recon for two months, he could still best some lowlife bandits.

As they got closer the bandits revealed themselves, they surrounded the two Outryders, one bandit, the leader, spoke, "Give us your money and you won't d..." before he even finished the sentence, Orion sent a knife through his chest. The bandits collapsed in on them, Orion sent two more knives, each one striking the heart of the aggressors. Haran had also sent a knife, but his struck a bandit right above the knee. There were still four bandits, two on Orion and two on Haran. These bandits were better than average, but still could not compete with the Orion and Haran. Orion dispatched his two with ease but decided to not intervene so he could see how Haran did against a real opponent. Orion had always known that

Haran was better than the average Recon, but now he saw how naturally good Haran really was with his axes, he sent the first bandit reeling with a deadly downward cut, killing him instantly. The second was much the same, with Haran showing his gracefulness with the axes.

"Leave him alive," Orion said over the ringing of Haran's blades on the frightened bandit's poorly balanced sword. Haran sent him reeling by sweeping his legs, as he was on the ground gasping for breath as he had been cut multiple times by Haran, Orion noticed something on his coat, an insignia of a white wolf. Orion knew every insignia for every fief, and there was no fief that had a wolf on it much less a white one, he checked the other bandits, same insignia.

Confused, he asked the bandit pointing to his insignia, "What is this," the bandit just responded with four words, the last he would ever speak, "Long live the wolf."

Orion looked confused by what that meant, but he had no time to think over it, Rowan the master horse breeder was waiting on him, and he was a busy man. By the time they got to the pasture where Rowan lived, it was early the next morning, they had to rest for most of the day before due to a deep cut Haran had gotten on his arm in his encounter with the bandits Rowan was an old, nice looking man who, as they walked into the stable said. "Ah, if it isn't my favorite Outryder and his daring new apprentice, please, lets have a drink before you take your pick of these fascinating creatures." Rowan said admiring his own creations.

They walked inside old man Rowan's house, and Haran noticed something about the old man's right eye. It never once moved with the left one, the old man had a fake eye. "Your eye, what happened to it?" Haran asked not knowing how offensive the question could be. Orion tried to shush him as to not offend the old man. However, Rowan just laughed,

"Oh, he is a true Outryder that one is." He said to Orion who cringed a little after the question. "Well son, I used to be quite the looker back in the day, much similar to you, and lets just say that the person who took my eye out wasn't doing it out of hate if you know what I mean." Haran not realizing what he meant looked at him skeptically. Rowan laughed, the classic old man cackle, slapped his knee and nudged Orion who had the slightest hint of a smile on his face.

Haran sat for a little while listening to the two of them catch up, but after thirty minutes of horse facts and boring Outryder paperwork, Haran ventured out of the house and into the stables. All of the horses looked like Ranger and Nova, but all of them were unique, one was brown in the head with a grey body, one was grey and black spotted, and another was brown and grey.

As he looked down the rows of stalls, one stood out to him, a pure grey horse with a strange looking white, ghostly figure under the horse's right eye. He went to pet the horse who responded with an exhale from his nose, he accepted the petting gratefully.

Soon after, Rowan and Orion followed him, knowing that they had spent too long talking. They walked into the stables where they saw Haran petting the pure grey horse.

"What's this one called," Haran asked after he saw them enter the stables.

"That there is the new Spirit, his ol' man was the best of the bunch, but I aint had a chance to test this Spirit yet," Rowan said, holding out an apple for the horse to eat.

"I want him," Haran responded, he did not know why, but he had already formed a connection with Spirit.

"Ok, why don't you take em for a test spin then," Rowan said, gesturing for him to saddle the horse up. After Haran got the saddle on and got him out of the stables, he could really test the horse's speed. As he was got out of the stables, he urged Spirit to a canter, then a gallop. The field was about half kilometer long and it seemed as in a matter of seconds, he had already crossed it. Spirit was lighting fast; it was almost as if he were gliding on the wind itself. His eyes were watery as he looked at the house that looked as if it were a speck of dust on the beauty of the rising sun. He was back in thirty seconds, "Ho-Ho-Ho, yeah, I definitely want this bad boy," Haran said excitedly to Rowan. Rowan was shocked at the speed of the horse, no horse he had ever trained had gone that fast, and he trained the fastest horses in the world.

"Just promise I can have him back when he gets too old, he will revolutionize the breeding world," Rowan said finally, kicking himself for not testing the horse earlier, he would have used it as the breeder.

They started traveling back to Norhall a few hours after Haran chose Spirit; Haran on his new horse, he smiled to himself, he was glad he had chosen that horse. He also wondered about that bandit attack the day before, why would they attack two heavily armed Outryders? What was that insignia all about? Where had he seen it before? And why did he have a feeling that this was not going to be good?

Chapter 12

Lottie had been training with Battlemaster Gilpin for about two months now; he had been able to hold his own a little with the Battlemaster at the start, but now he could best Gilpin thirty percent of the time, with his blistering speed and precision. Lottie had gone to the canyon eleven times now, each time studying how the wolves moved, fought and hunted; he was amazed at the majestic creatures and their abilities. Lottie asked Battlemaster Gilpin if Ella could join them in training, since she was also very capable with the sword. Gilpin, owing Ella a favor, and respecting Lottie, let her train with them. After they started training, they started to become close, between sharing classes and training with the Battlemaster every day, they began to connect on a more personal level, almost intimate. Ella was beautiful after all, her light brown eyes gleaming upon her tanned skin and her blond hair as if she had been crafted to perfection by a greater being. Lottie was big, muscular, and handsomely rugged in an attractive way, so it made perfect sense for there to be attraction between the two young people. However, for now, Gilpin did not approve, he had started seeing the liking of the two children and told Lottie to keep that out of their training. He had seen excellent fighters go down the wrong path because of a woman, and he wouldn't let that happen to his new protégé; at least until he knew what this Ella girl was after. After their training session, Gilpin called Lottie and Ella over.

"It's about time for both of you to pick your horses", he said as he started walking to the stables. Full of fully trained battle horses bred for speed and power. There were three free horses in the back, a pure black, a brown and white spotted, and a pure white. Lottie automatically gravitated towards the black one, and Ella towards the brown and white. Lottie due to its menacing appearance, and Ella because it looked like her grandfathers' horse, Skipper. Lottie named his horse Midnight, due to its resemblance to the time; Ella named her horse Skipper after her grandfather's.

After they chose their horse, a messenger came from Norhall Castle, "Battlemaster! Battlemaster! The Baron needs you!" he called. Gilpin saddled up his horse, Blaze, and gestured for Lottie and Ella to follow on their horses. As they galloped to the castle Lottie grasping for dear life from this being his first horse ride. After they got to Castle Norhall, Lottie retched due to all the jostling of a barreling battle horse. Ella faired a little better off since she had been riding since she was a little girl. They went up to the keep where Gilpin went inside the Baron's office, leaving them outside of the door.

Lottie suggested they head into town, where Lottie saw Heide buying bread from the bakery, her beautiful red hair flowing with the wind. He had always liked Heide, she was always nice to him and she was always fair when it came to his arguments with Haran.

"Heide," he called her over, she looked around not knowing who called her, it was a familiar voice, she thought. After she finally saw who it was that called her name, she went over to him, however she did not know who the blond girl he was with was.

Whoever she was, she was beautiful, her golden locked tied into a perfectly tight bun Heide thought as she approached them, "Hey Lottie, what are you doing in town, aren't you supposed to be at the Battleschool?"

Lottie responded gesturing towards Ella, "Ah yes, Ella and I were training with Gilpin, when a strange messenger talked to him about the Baron needing him, so we went with him and ended up here."

"oh, sounds pretty serious..." Heide responded worriedly.

"It is, and I am very sorry, but we must get going," Ella interrupted hastily. Obviously jealous of this new girl in front of her.

Heide responded with a cold, "Who are you again?" Ella was a little taken aback, but before she could respond, Lottie interrupted, explaining how they met and who she was.

"Anyways, Lottie have you talked to Lottie since he became an Outryder." Heide said seemingly proud for her friend.

"Actually yes, we had a little scuffle in a tournament a month or two back at the tournament," Lottie said trying to avoid the fact that he fought the boy.

"Wait what, why would you fight him? What did he say?" Heide asked, genuinely worried about what happened.

"Nothing really, it was regulated, he is fine, but he did give me a run until he lost his cool," Lottie said recalling the events. Heide looked at Lottie in a new light, maybe this Battleschool had changed Lottie. Maybe his rage and anger that Heide hated so much about Lottie had been channeled. But what did he mean when he said Haran lost his cool? Haran never lost his cool, she thought to herself. But before she could ask Lottie, Battlemaster Gilpin approached, Heide swiftly exited, knowing he had to talk to his two apprentices.

He waited until she was out of earshot and continued, "Get packed."

"What for?" Lottie questioned.

He responded with a question of his own," You ever raid a bandit camp before?"

It was half past noon when they had gotten ready to leave for the bandit camp; apparently, Orion and Haran had gotten attacked by some bandits at the border of Norhall going to

Anjagor fief. And, after some investigating, they had found a bandit camp only a kilometer from where they were attacked.

Lottie was excited, but the only thing he dreaded was trusting his life in the hands of Orion and especially Haran. From Orion's scouting it wasn't a big bandit camp, but it was sizable enough for a six-person raid party. The party consisted of Gilpin, Lottie, Ella, Orion, Haran, and Lyra.

Gilpin would have brought more experienced fighters, but he figured this would give his apprentices much need experience, and if something too bad were to happen, there was always Orion and himself there to stop it. Baron Ligate told the Battlemaster that the two companies were to meet outside the castle at one, so after they had gathered all their things, they had an hour to spare.

As they rode into town to pick up fresh meat for their dinner, they already saw the Outryders doing exactly that. Gilpin approached the Outryders, "One step ahead of me as always I see," Gilpin said jokingly as he shook hands with Orion. He had always come to rely on Orion, not to say they were friends by any means; Orion was always a recluse in that way.

Orion simply nodded and gestured towards their horses, " You ready to head out, or did you want to wait until nightfall," he said it in a way that he wouldn't offend the Battlemaster, but to also let him know that his time was valuable. They set on their way northwest past the Wolf's Tail and on the main road to Anjagor.

Haran and Lottie said little to each other on the way, but Ella and Lyra however, talked essentially the whole way. Shiva was still small enough to fit in Haran's satchel, but Scarlett had to follow behind the party, striking up an immediate conversation between the girls. They stopped at sunset, about a kilometer from where the bandit camp was.

"Alright you all, we are going to stop for tonight, for now, gather firewood and set up the camp, Orion and I are going to check out this bandit camp," Gilpin said addressing the children.

The girls started to set up camp, and unpacking, chatting along the way. Haran took Shiva out of his satchel to let her stretch her legs, and he went on to gathering firewood with Lottie.

"Hey," Haran said awkwardly, Lottie just nodded, he didn't necessarily like Haran since their little incident at Calcore Canyon, he looked at the long scars on his arms then back at Haran, then back at his arms. And even though he won the tournament, he knew that Haran was his own true enemy in that fight.

Haran grabbed a giant log almost eight feet long, he didn't necessarily need it, but he thought he might as well grab it. However, it was just too big for him to carry, so he dropped it on the ground in front of him, "Ugh, why are you so useless," Lottie said insultingly.

"What is your problem, Lottie," Haran responded.

They had never really addressed what happened at the canyon, so it all came flooding out of Lottie at this moment, "You Haran, you are weak, you were too weak to beat me at the tournament, and you were too weak to save me in that canyon the day I got these scars," Lottie said motioning to his scars.

"Lottie, the canyon was not my fault, there is no way you can put that on me," Haran responded a little too severely. Lottie only saw red, and if not for the girls coming up to tell them the camp was set up, he probably would have drawn his swords.

Lottie gave Haran a look that said, "This isn't over" and Haran's steely gaze replied "I'm ready when you are," as they went back to the camp with the two beautiful girls.

Gilpin and Orion arrived at the bandit camp a little after sunset, where they saw two dozen bandits milling around. If this were the same bandit camp that the bandits that attacked Haran and Orion on the road were from, they would not be the greatest swordsmen. There was no one on watch, which surprised Orion, even though they were lowlife bandits with probably little to no education, he still would have figured they would know enough to defend themselves at night. Orion had figured with this size of a bandit party, they would probably be going after something larger than some lonely travelers, they would probably hit a farm next, steal all the animals, and maybe destroy the farmer's crops for fun. Good thing they were here to stop that before it happened Orion thought.

It was an hour later by the time they had gotten familiar with the lay of the land, the camp was at the bottom of a slight hill in the middle of a forest, a fallen tree in the middle that the bandits sat on, a giant outcrop of rocks to the left, and plenty of trees, meaning plenty of cover for the Outryders to pick some off before the attack. However, it also meant plenty of cover for the bandits in case of an attack.

By the time they got back, the children had already set up camp and got a little fire started. For dinner, they had rabbit stew made by Orion and, surprisingly, he was an excellent cook. With Lottie even going for four bowls before he was done. Soon after dinner, they had all went to bed; Haran had the first watch. He behind a rock outcrop that kept him hidden from the road, and he sat for about four hours with Shiva, just listening to the sound of rabbits scurrying from bush to bush, and the wind rustling the trees around him.

After some time, he heard something a little off with the sounds around him, just the slightest, most unnoticeable sound of a leaf scrunching under the boot of a very silent intruder near their camp. As he waited to see if the intruder would show themselves, a hand came out of the shadows behind him, seizing his shoulder, he jumped up ready to fight whatever this mysterious figure could be.

"Relax Haran it's me, I am just coming to join you," Lyra said worried that he might preemptively strike.

Haran sat back down and scratched his head in embarrassment, "yeah, yeah, I knew that I knew that."

Lyra let out a soft laugh, Haran looked at her with a frown, "It's not funny you know, what if you were a bandit, or Lottie, or someone," Haran said.

She stopped laughing, acknowledging his point, "What is it with you two, you seem like you don't like each other. And even at the tournament you seemed as if your were not yourself around him." she said sincerely curious.

"Yes well, we don't, it's a long story, but to sum it up, Lottie is a bully, and a cheat, we used to be friend, until one day when he fell into Calcore Canyon and blamed me for it," Haran said softly.

Lyra noticed he was hurt by this and decided against pushing forward, "What do you think of Ella," she asked in a way that only a jealous girl would.

"She is fine I guess, you two really seemed to really hit it off though," Haran said, changing the subject from him to her.

"Yeah, she is very nice, and I think we could be close friends one day," Lyra finished, looking into the starry sky above.

Haran yawned, it had been a long day, "Here Haran, I'll take over for you, you only got about ten more minutes until it's my turn anyway," Lyra said as she looked at the boy, never breaking eye contact, she admired him, he was a natural with the axe, and she already knew he would be far better than she would ever be at them.

Haran thanked her, but he didn't leave yet; he just wanted to stay there and talk to her all night. He eventually did get up after his ten minutes were up, and went off to sleep. "That boy," Lyra said softly cursing to herself for even offering the shift change.

Chapter 13

They got up at sunrise the next day, Orion had planned to set up the three Outryders around the camp so that they could pick off some bandits before they launched the full attack. As they arrived, he signaled for Haran to veer left and Lyra right. Haran hid behind a tree and Lyra did the same. Orion took the big outcrop because he would stay with Gilpin and his apprentices to draw the largest group of bandits toward them. That's when Haran and Lyra would come from behind the bandits while they were engaged with Orion's group and hit them unexpectedly. It was a simple plan, but Orion knew if the plan were to be too complicated, things were more likely to go wrong. As they had planned, Orion's knife went first, followed by two more from two different angles, each striking true to their targets. Two more knives come from Orion in a matter of only two seconds, and two more go down. about this time the bandits figured out what was happening and bolted for cover, two knives thudded against the fallen tree they used for shelter. With only five down, Orion cursed slightly under his breath, he was hoping he could get at least eight before they even thought about close combat. They stopped throwing, but each still has one ready to throw if a bandit were to peak their head up. After about ten minutes, the bandits made their move, moving towards Orion's group. Four more went down before they made it to their next shelter, which was a slight dip in the ground perfectly sized to conceal them from the rain of projectiles. One bandit peaked his head up and had his hair cut from a razor-sharp blade as he went back down. Orion signaled to Gilpin to make his move, following in suit. Haran saw the small group of attackers pushing toward the bandits and called over to Lyra, but she had already noticed and was also pushing in. The bandits peak their head up just in time to see the attackers pushing them and get out of the positioning the natural ditch gave. Gilpin, Lottie, and Ella led the charge on the bandits, they couldn't let the Outryders have all the fun.

They were outnumbered three to one, but by the time they clashed it seemed more even, four bandits went down instantly, and after about ten seconds, that's when Haran and Lyra got there, killing two more. It was nine against six now and the bandits realized they were outmatched, so they broke off, trying to get away before they were killed. Haran and Lottie both got one each in the back, and the other bandits were caught by the others before they could get away.

With seven prisoners, the group took an hour to tie them all up in a line and started walking back to Norhall Castle stopping at a nearby stream to clean up the blood. "Your boy over there is a real natural huh," Orion said to Gilpin gesturing towards Lottie who was cleaning up at the river.

"Yeah, so is yours," Gilpin responded, the boy fought gracefully and composed under pressure. Any master could see that each boy was a force to be reckoned with in their own right. "And those axes, he is a natural with those, and they are very effective."

Orion just nodded, distracted by thoughts about the bandits that had first attacked them on the road, about the dying breath of a poor bandit, and about the small wolf insignia on their variety of clothing. He walked up to the bandits, who were tied to a tree and being watched closely by Haran and Lyra. He turned one over and looked at his chest, but there was nothing there, he looked at another, nothing, and another, nothing. That is when he realized, these were different from the bandits that attacked them on the road.

Everyone walked over, noticing his confusion, "What's wrong Orion," Gilpin asked worriedly.

Orion looked up, his face drained with the thought, "I think we got the wrong guys."

There were a chorus of questions that rang out from the small group, "What do you mean?"

"How?"

"Wrong bandits?"

He gestured for silence, "All of the bandits that attacked me and Haran had a specific insignia of a wolf's head on their chest, these bandits however, do not."

Trying to prove his theory, he sketched up the insignia as best as he could remember and then walked over to the bandits again, "Do you recognize this symbol?"

The bandits shook their heads, as he had thought, there was no relation between these bandits and the mysterious group that had attacked them on the road, these ones were probably just the run of the mill poor bandit looking for a living through robbery, the others were more skilled and he had a feeling, more dangerously sinister.

Gilpin gave him a questioning look, "I will explain to you when we report to the Baron," Orion whispered quietly, trying not to let the children hear.

They didn't speak the whole way to the castle, even if there was much to talk about. Haran just simply played with Shiva, who, had almost developed her own personality. When they returned to Castle Norhall, Orion and Battlemaster Gilpin entered Baron Ligate's office to report. As they finished Ligate asked, "What do you mean, 'not the right bandits' they were only a kilometer away from where you were attacked, what other bandits would there be?"

"Listen, I know it sounds unbelievable, but the bandits that attacked Haran and I on the road were far better than the ones we took as prisoners, and the ones that attacked us had a small wolf symb…"

Orion was cut off by Battlemaster Gilpin, "Orion, this sounds like a lot of speculation to me, just accept it man, we got the bad guys."

Ligate nodded in response, "Respectfully I would have to agree with Gilpin on this one Orion, just congratulate yourself on the good work and keep it up."

"Well respectfully Baron, the only people of higher rank than me in this country are the Outryder Commander and King Nigel himself, so respectfully I would like to resume what I was saying please." Orion said calmly emphasizing the word respectfully as to show his superiority.

Speechless, Ligate gestured for him to continue, "Thank you," Orion said, giving it a second then continued with his previous statement, "As I was saying, the bandits that attacked us on the road had a small wolf symbol on their chest, and when I questioned one about it he responded with 'long live the wolf', now do you know of anything with a wolf in recent times?"

He was addressing Ligate, but it was Gilpin who responded, "Orion, come on, you can't listen to the words of a dying bandit whose life revolved around killing and stealing."

Before Orion could respond Ligate interrupted, "Ok Orion, its dually noted and it will be reported to the King as soon as possible," Orion nodded his appreciation and left the room.

"What happened? What did you mean when you said those weren't the right bandits," Haran asked as Orion walked into the cabin; Lyra had gone to check up on a report of three dead chickens in Calcore Canyon.

"Well, what did you notice about the bandits that had attacked us on the road and how did they differ from the ones we just fought," Orion asked, trying to test Haran's ability to pay attention to detail.

"Ummm, the ones that attacked us on the road were better than the others I guess," Haran said, pondering what he had noticed, but it all seemed like a blur. "Anything else? Anything different with say what they were wearing," Orion said trying to engage Haran's brain.

"Ah yes that's right, the bandits that attacked us had a grey, refined furs on, whereas the ones today wore tattered cloth in no specific color," Haran said, recalling he had seen the bandits with a combination of dark greys and light grey furs on.

Orion nodded giving the gesture for Haran to continue, he thought for a minute or so then finally came up with an answer, "Ah yes the symbols, the bandits that attacked us on the road had an insignia of a wolf stitched on their chests, I assume it is some type of insignia for a fief like the Dalhurst's stars or Norhall's crossed swords."

Orion nodded, impressed at Haran's reasoning, for it was exactly what he thought, "I thought the same thing, but..." he went into his room, found a book and flipped to the page with what looked like every insignia for every fief, "As you can see, there is not one symbol that resembles a wolf in all of Anjagor's thirty-five fiefs." Haran nodded looking through all the symbols, trying to piece together what the symbol on the bandits was, but he was stumped.

After about ten minutes Orion finally said, "From the little that we know Haran I have a gut feeling that the attack on us was not just some random attack, but it was premeditated by someone who knew where we were going."

That night in Calcore Canyon a small group of ten people in a combination of grey and white furs approached the same dozen wolves that Lottie had started seeing with Gilpin. The wolves, sitting outside their cave got up as they saw the group approaching, ready to attack any traveler that dared enter their domain.

They relaxed a little, for the leader, a well-built, muscular man in his late forties, had been visiting them for years now trying to learn their ways. The wolves trusted this man, but they had just figured out that one of their kind was pregnant. They could not take any risk, so the alpha met them at the about ten meters from where the young mother sat, daring the man to step forward. He wisely did not, he was only there to observe, this was their domain, and he knew was subject to their reign.

"Observe, my dearest friends, he is near, he who will finally bring us back." the man spoke, a voice of a powerful, charismatic man, one who knows his place and revels in it. There was a resounding applause that followed his words, he held of a hand for silence, "These are the roots of the coming savior, and when he finally comes, we finally get our revenge!"

The applause shook echoed through the walls of Calcore Canyon and the leader looked up to see a sliver of the moon above him, "Soon," he whispered to the stars above, "I can feel him coming. Soon."

Chapter 14

※

Lottie noticed that his favorite wolf Gai, as he called her, was pregnant soon after he and the Outryders had taken on the bandit camp, and he had been taking as best care of her as frequently possible. The alpha wolf, Fenir, as Gilpin had deemed him, allowed only Lottie to get near the soon to be mother for some reason.

Lottie would get her water every day and take her food whenever he could, they had formed an unbreakable bond during her pregnancy and he even considered taking her home, but Gilpin would never let him take a wolf away from their pack.

The festival was coming up and Heide sent him a letter stating that, she planned for all of Lottie's old friends to get together at midday in the Malen Plains for a picnic. It would be good to see her again, he thought, he had not seen her since before they took on the bandit camp; Heide was always so understanding when it came to his feud with Haran and would always be fair when they fought.

He wrote her back asking if he could take Ella with him, he knew that they had not gotten off to a good start, but he was hoping that they could bond as Ella and Lyra had done. As he thought about it, Haran and Lyra will be there as well, and the last time it talked to Haran, it did not go to good. He pushed the thought out of his mind and went on with his training for that day; he will deal with it when time comes, until then all he could do was anxiously wait.

It was now a week until the festival, and after training every single day all day, Haran was ready to see his old friend again. He and Lyra already had already asked Orion for permission and were just waiting for their break.

They had been training harder every day since the whole bandit incident, but Orion always said, "Perfection is a combination of hard work and skill, but you cannot have the latter without a lot of the former."

Haran hated Orion's quotes because they always made him do more work, but had already seen much improvement due to the amount of work. At only three and a half months into his training, he was already unknowingly one of the best hands to hand combatant in all the Recons.

Although he is a brilliant fighter, he struggles a little with the most necessary part of the Outryder's training, silence. Every single day he practices, but every single time, he fails to get past Orion or Lyra, he steps on a twig, crunches some leaves, one time he even walking into a low hanging tree branch.

Today, was essentially the same, three hours of failure after failure, each time taking a new route, every time getting the slightest bit farther than the last. He could not figure how Orion and Lyra did it with such ease, he was rightfully aggravated, and Orion saw that on his face after he found him moving from a bush thirty meters away, "You know, I was worse at this than you when I started as a Recon."

"Really?" Haran had always thought Orion was the best, even when he was a Recon.

"Yes, I was terrible, but my master told me one thing that made me as I am today, he said 'It is impossible to maintain silence being in the woods, but to maintain silence you must become a part of the woods,' so become the woods Haran and use your cloak." They decided to stop for today, because there was only about an hour left in the day and they still had to check the snares.

The next day, when Haran had finished his training with Lyra, he was itching to practice being silent again, but Orion was not anywhere to be seen and, when he thought about it, Haran had not seen him all day. He asked Lyra about it, and she responded with, "Orion went to the castle library to do some research on something. I don't remember, but you will probably find him there."

He thanked her and headed off to the castle library. Lady Usrea was in there as always; Haran waved and went over to where he saw his master with a-meter-high pile of books beside him, "There you are Orion, I have been looking for you, I wanted to try out what you told me yesterday," he said.

Orion looked up from his books with a face rarely seen on Orion, fear, "Haran, I think you might want to look at this," he said, pointing to the lines he was reading.

It was a prophecy that read:

> *Tale discovered much too late*
> *To turn the tables or change the fate.*
> *On the shortest day and the longest night,*
> *the savior born a wolf of white.*
> *The mother's death will mark the time,*
> *when revenge is at its prime.*
> *The day the savior reaches age;*
> *The death of one lead to fits of rage.*
> *Two sons battle on a canyon's edge*
> *where the final blow will drive the wedge.*
> *Friends will try, and friends will fail.*
> *The order of the wolf will prevail.*

"I don't understand, it's just some random prophecy it doesn't mean anything," Haran said.

"And that's what I said thirty years ago in your shoes when we were researching old prophecies for a different case," Orion responded as he grabbed the book and started walking out of the library Haran at his heel.

"But think about it boy, *on the shortest day and the longest night*, the shortest day and the longest night is the winter solstice. And *the savior born a wolf of white*; the bandits that attacked us could have been worshipping this *wolf of white*, that would explain the 'long live the wolf' that the bandits said right before he died."

It took a while for Haran to respond, but when he did, he said, "So if all of this is true then we only have six days until the 'savior' is born. How do we know it has not happened yet, or will happen sometime in the far future?"

Orion responded instantly, "Listen Haran, we discovered this prophecy's ties to our problems only six days before it says the savior will be born, in prophetic terms that is almost impossible to stop, or *change the fate.*"

He did not want to admit it, but Orion was right, this prophecy was talking about the winter solstice this year, and according to the prophecy, there was nothing they could do about it.

Chapter 15

Haran woke up in fits of sweat, he had been thinking about the prophecy all night long, and how he could locate where the "savior" would be born. He looked over the prophecy meticulously since he brought it home from the library, he knew every space, every dot, and every dirt stain on that paper, but every time he looked at it, nothing changed.

He knew, that somehow, he was a part of the story, but he did not know which part, would he have to prepare himself for an inevitable fight, or would he be the one that dies. Either way, he knew that it would change his life as he knew it; that somehow, the people that had tried to kill him and Orion on that gravel road, would win, and he could not believe it.

It was now that day, he had spent the last six days trying to figure out the solution to the prophecy, but to no avail. For now, he and Lyra had to get to Malen plains, he did not want to break his promise and upset Heide, because he couldn't die in the prophecy if he is dead before it even started. As he saddled up Spirit he looked over to his lion, Shiva, she had grown to the point where she couldn't fit in his satchel anymore, so he decided against taking her.

"Ready to go Haran," he heard Lyra call from the porch of the cabin. She had already saddle up Ranger and was waiting impatiently for him. She also decided against taking Scarlett with her; she took Scarlett everywhere, so she decided to give her a break for today.

As they rode through the winding trails of Fuestres Woods, Haran began thinking about a time not long ago when he hadn't had to deal with death prophecies and wolf cults. He hoped that today, with Heide and all the others, he could go back to the time with no stress or worries.

Lottie and Ella were the first ones there, which made sense, the Battleschool was very close to the Lightbringer, the place where Heide said to meet at. The Lightbringer was a tree in the middle of Malen Plains that was struck by lightning and shattered to a million tiny pieces, and it was a perfect place for a picnic. The grass was surprisingly well kept in this area, because all the grass within a kilometer of the Battleschool had to be mandatorily cut so they could see any attackers approaching from a distance. Also, it was not far from a clump of strawberries growing, so it made for an excellent day out.

Heide showed up right at midday with an assortment of food for the children, pies, fresh bread, soups, and cooked mutton. She greeted Lottie and Ella and they began setting up the picnic. Ten minutes after, Bertrand showed up, and five minutes after that Haran and Lyra.

After all their introduction, Lyra and Ella exchanged a short laugh. Heide had yet to meet Lyra, so she started a conversation, "Soo, how do you know Haran," she asked to Lyra, but it was Haran that responded, "I told you already, she trains under Orion with me."

As he heard the name Lottie's rage was already festering, he still remembers getting out of that river soaking wet and having to walk home. Ella noticed his sudden switch in mood at the name and grabbed his arm, reminding him that he was to behave today.

Heide saw the gesture and, jealous, changed to subject to Lyra and Ella, "It seems as if you know each other already, how you met?"

"Well, it's a funny story actually..." Lyra responded, but he already saw the boys getting bored and changed course a little.

"Why don't us girls get the stuff ready and we can talk about it, while the boys go gather some strawberries."

Haran smiled at the suggestion and gestured for Lottie and Bertrand to follow him. They got on their horses and set off towards the strawberry bushes.

"Nice horse you got there Lottie, what's its names?" asked Bertrand.

"Midnight," Lottie responded as if that name was just a poetic masterpiece.

Haran was about to make a joke and then held his tongue, he could not mess up Heide's day with their petty squabbles. "How has it been Lottie, what you been up to since seeing you last," He said distracting himself from the way to obvious joke.

"A whole lot of training, and you," Lottie said, also trying not to start anything today.

"likewise," Haran said.

"You learn any magic yet as an Outryder" Lottie said making a hand gesture that vaguely resembles what Lottie thought magic would look like.

Lottie said it jokingly, but Haran knew it was meant to be degrading, "No, there is no such thing as magic, but I have gotten pretty good with these axes here," he said unsheathing them from their sheaths on his back.

Lottie didn't like Haran in the slightest, but he could appreciate a fine warrior, "As I saw, you were really surprisingly good in the field."

Haran took this as a high form of flattery, and decided to keep the ball rolling, "You're not too bad yourself, I see you also enjoy the double scabbard yourself," he said gesturing toward the two simple swords hung at his waist.

By this time, they had reached the bushes, and all dismounted respectively, "Yeah, they are the best weapons for attacking, so it was an obvious choice," Lottie said as he put a handful of strawberries in the bucket he brought, they were a little past harvest date, but they would still be very delicious.

"I prefer defense, waiting for the opponent to make a mistake, then striking as if a snake had just come out of hiding," Haran said, but before Lottie could even respond, following up with. "We should really spar sometime; I would like to see the result of that."

Lottie gave it a minute or so then responded, "Me too Haran, me too,"

By the time they had gotten back, the girls had already fully set up and were waiting for the boys so they could eat. They seemed to know each other a bit more, sharing laughs as the boys approached. "What is so funny," Haran asked, as he sat down in between Heide and Lyra.

Heide responded, "oh nothing, I was just telling these two the story when you and Lottie both fell into the Wolf's Tail when we were young,"

"No not that one, it is so embarrassing," Lottie interjected.

"What, I think it's cute, you two boys trying to log roll across the river," Lyra said.

"It wouldn't have been cute if you were there, that water is freezing cold," Haran said. Everyone laughed and they began sharing more stories of their younger years. Heide trying to get a rat to do tricks, Bertrand and his many falls over his own shoes, or a rock on the ground. Lottie and Haran fighting a rabid dog in a dark alley to save the others. The memories flooding through them, reminiscing over old times, they were all so gleeful and so unaware at what was about to unfold.

They sat there for hours telling those stories, until dusk broke, when Lottie and Haran started a fire. After they got the fire started, Haran sat back down, "What about you two Lyra and Ella," Bertrand said, "We all know each other, but we don't know much about yall."

Lyra gave her story, her parents death, her moving to Norhall, how she met Orion, and eventually how she got here today; there was an echo of sadness from the group when they heard about the death of her parents, they hadn't really known their parents, and it was probably worse to know them and lose them than to lose them before you know them.

Ella started sharing now, her mom not being there most of her life, and her dad dying at the Athonian hands, how she came here, and eventually getting to the part about training with Battlemaster Gilpin, "... we go to Calcore Canyon to train with the wolves, Gilpin says it is a way to master the art of combat, Lottie actually, has grown quite attached to one after her pregnancy..."

Haran raised his eyebrows in response to that statement, so he decided to press a little, "When is she due?"

"Should be soon, either tonight or tomorrow, at least that's what Gilpin thinks," Ella responded, peaked by his interest in the pregnancy.

"Tonight, the solstice?" he said, getting up from the spot he was sitting and moving Heide's head off of his lap, "We really must be going Lyra," he said, she nodded in agreement.

"Speaking of Gai, I really need to be there during the birth, if you don't mind Heide," Lottie said.

"Ok, that's totally fine, great night you guys, see you next year," she said it jokingly, but she was genuinely hurt by the boys' sudden disappearance.

Haran and Lyra were quick to get leave, and when they left earshot of the small group, Lyra said, "We got to find that wolf."

"Yep, this might be our only chance, we have to hurry," Haran said as he got onto Spirit.

Lyra understood now, and nodded her head, and after they were out of the groups view, they both urged their horses into a full gallop.

Chapter 16

✿

It was four hours until midnight when Lottie arrived at Calcore Canyon. Gilpin briefed him of what happened since he was gone, her water just broke, which means they needed to get started right away.

As Lottie crouched down next to her favorite creature, he felt a little sad, she was once a lively thing, now she looked as if she were sick. The birthing process started now, and Gilpin went to get a doctor from the village, who had performed births before, Lottie's only job was to be there to make sure nothing terrible happened in the process.

Gilpin came back with the doctor, Rewet, about thirty minutes later, and told Lottie and Gilpin to relax; that it would be a few hours. Gilpin and Lottie got a campfire going, to warm up a little bit, there was no need for them to be waiting in the cold for hours, especially when there was nothing more than they could do.

"Do you think I could keep one Battlemaster," Lottie asked, he had grown attached to Gai, and would like to have one of her pups as proof of that.

"It depends Lottie, I don't know if she will allow you to take one of her newly born puppies," Gilpin responded nonchalantly as he waited for Rewet to call them over for updates.

He did, around the eleventh hour, "Battlemaster Gilpin, I think you should come see this,"

Gilpin got up and waited a couple seconds, his eyes not adjusted to the darkness after staring at a fire for two hours, and then walk over with Lottie following close behind.

Lottie looked at the doctor's face, and saw pure despair, he looked down and saw, a pool of blood around Gai, his favorite creature in the entire world. She was near death on the ground half a meter away.

"What does this mean," he asked with bewilderment.

"Well, it could mean two things, but neither of them good, one the mother dies with no offspring, two the mother dies with one offspring that is very weak and will probably die shortly after," Rewet said, not knowing the connection that Lottie had formed with Gai.

"So, you are saying, either way, the only job that you were meant to do is to keep her and the cubs alive, and she will die in my arms," Lottie said, rage building inside, the only thing in this world that had not failed him is about to die with him being able to do nothing about it. Gilpin stepped in between the two people, he knew Lottie could be hot headed, so he decided to save the poor doctor from his apprentice's wrath.

"Listen son, it is nature, and not everything can be perfect in nature, that's the sad truth, all we can do now is to help the mother to deliver her cub or her whole life will have been pointless," Rewet said, very sympathetically.

And so they did; with only thirty minutes left to live, the cub popped out at twenty-nine. And Gai died in Lottie's arms. The cub was the biggest cub Rewet had ever seen, he weighed about three pounds and started whining as soon as he emerged from his mother womb. After Rewet had gotten all the blood off of the cub, they saw that it was a male, they also saw that the cub's fur was pure white, which should have been impossible, the mother was grey, and the father was jet black.

As Lottie got up from next to the dead wolf, he walked over to her cub, the only other reminder of the deceased, and took it from the doctor, he looked at Battlemaster Gilpin and then the wolf, and then to Gilpin.

Gilpin knew exactly what he was say and said, "Of course Lottie" there was a pause of about three seconds, "you can keep him."

Haran and Lyra rode hard to the cabin, pushing their horses to near exhaustion as they entered Fuestres Woods. Orion heard the hoofbeats outside, he knew something was up. There would have been no reason to be riding that fast in these woods unless you knew where you were going.

"What has happened," he asked as they skidded their horses in front of the cabin porch. They explained everything, and without even saying a word, Orion saddled up and started towards the canyon, it might be too late however, he thought looking at the moon almost directly above his head.

"What do you plan on doing when we get there," Haran asked, looking at his master for guidance, and this time, the was the one time that there was no response or a witty comment, there was no answer.

They arrived at the canyon three hours before twelve, but they still had to find the wolf in the large place. It was an impossible task, especially since Haran didn't know his bearings in the darkness. Even if they did find the wolves in time, they would still have to figure out a way to stop the birth with Lottie and Gilpin there. They split up, to cover more ground in the vast canyon, searching everywhere for any source of sound, a cub crying, a wolf howling with celebration, but there was nothing. Until there was, half past twelve, Haran was nearing the end of the canyon when he heard the sound, faint, demonic sounding chants. He immediately threw himself against the canyon walls, blending in with the shadows, and trusting that his cloak would hide him from any unwanted observers.

"*Lupus Vivat, Lupus Vivat, Lupus Vivat,*" the chants were getting closer, to the point he could understand the word, it was an ancient, long forgotten language that he somewhat recognized. As he sunk deeper into the shadows, a light was flashing around the bend, his heart was beating so fast and loud in his chest that he thought they would hear him before they ever saw him.

When they rounded the bend, Haran saw them, around twenty men, each one in a wolf shaped grey mask and a grey pelt on their shoulders. The center of the group was holed out and it looked as if they were carrying something big in the center. Someone stood in front of the circle with a torch to light the way, both his mask and pelt were white, marking him as the leader. He couldn't see the face of the leader, but he did seem oddly familiar and he couldn't wrap his head around it.

They were only three meters away, and he tried to keep every muscle in his body still because if he even moved in the slightest someone would hear him. As they rounded the final bend, which led to the end of the canyon, Haran let out a sigh of relief. He waited ten minutes to make sure they did not come back while he was moving and made the decision to see what they were up to. However, when he rounded the bend, he saw nothing but a dark wall of rocks in his way.

Chapter 17

❈

"And you are sure that they just disappeared from the canyon no signs of any escape route," Orion asked after Haran gave his full report the next morning.

"Yes sir, as I said, they went past me, turning the corner chanting 'Lupus Vivat' and ten minutes after, they were gone."

Orion wrote it down, "Ok I will investigate where they could have escaped to during the lost ten minutes. For now though, this needs to be kept very quiet." Haran had already said that Battlemaster Gilpin and his apprentices were doing something with wolves. If he was in on whatever this was, Orion wouldn't trust anyone apart from the Outryder commander and the King himself, and until he had more to report, all he could do was pry a little bit more.

"Solid work Haran, I will look into it, for now, continue your training," Orion said as he saddled up his horse, Nova, to go to Calcore Canyon. Haran was awestruck, Orion had never complimented him before, and he knew how much that meant for his master to say that. Haran walked outside to get a breath of fresh air, recalling all those events in such vivid detail kind of scared him.

THUNK-THUNK-THUNK. He practiced his knife throwing for about an hour, until he decided to see what Lyra was up to.

"Hey super spy, how you are doing," Lyra said as she was practicing on a wooden dummy.

"Actually, not that great," he said and after a little pause he continued, "Would you want to go on a walk?"

"Would I ever," she said sheathing her weapons onto her back.

"Soo, what seems to be the problem," she asked when they reached the edge of the clearing.

"I'm scared Lyra, all of these prophecies and secret wolf gods and death, it scares me. Last night, when we were talking about the old days, I thought back to when the only bad thing that happened in my life was occasionally falling into rivers, now it's just so…"

"Haran, all of us are scared, I am, that's for sure, but that's a part of the Outryder ways, and all you can do now is enjoy the moment for what it is," Lyra said looking into his sea green eyes and his handsomely rugged face.

Haran stopped at the very edge of Fuestres Woods, he looked at the raven-haired girl, into her deep brown eyes, and her beautiful face, leaned in to kiss the girl; her eyes grew wide as if she were about to warn him of something behind him. Before she could though, he was struck in the head from behind, rendering him unconscious.

Haran woke up tied to a tree near where he was hit, he was confused how he got there, and then he remembered that he was talking with Lyra. LYRA, what happened to Lyra. He immediately reached for his axes, but there was nothing there.

He looked around, trying to figure out a way to get out of the tight knot he was tied to the tree with. Nothing. He thought about what they would do to Lyra if he were to not save her. Whoever they were that is. After about ten minutes of struggling he realized that he and Lyra came with their pets, so he called gently for Shiva. He heard rustling in bushes about twenty meters away, and when Shiva came out of the bushes towards Haran tentatively, he thanked whatever gods there was above. "Hey baby," Haran said comfortingly, "I know you are scared, but please help he out here." Shiva, somehow understanding, started chewing on the rope gluing Haran to the tree. This was the first time he realized how big Shiva really was; sitting down as he was, Shiva was actually taller than Haran by an inch or so. Haran figured all lions were built this way, but Shiva was only a few months old. When Shiva finished biting through the rope that held him, Haran let out a sign of relief and rolled his wrist to get back circulation. Haran looked at Shiva and said, "Listen, you stay here, I can't have you getting hurt on me.

Haran snuck his way to the edge of the clearing where he saw Lyra tied to a tree similar to how he was, but she was still unconscious. He looked around to see 7 bandits seven figures around the clearing, obviously looking for Orion. "How do they know that we live here?" Haran asked himself. He snuck around the clearing, circling to where Lyra was located, hiding behind a bush some five meters away. She was guarded by one bandit, one of the bandits from the camp two months ago. How did they get out of the dungeon, he thought to himself. He figured he could take this one out without his weapons, but the rest would be a different story. He decided to risk it since he couldn't see his weapons anywhere. Getting up, he crawled his way until he was a meter from the bandit, he then switched into a crouched position and finally stood up fully. With one punch, he knocked to bandit out cold, stealing his poorly weighted sword in hopes to defend himself from the other bandits who, would eventually come back to check on their companion. However, Haran didn't care, once he got Lyra free, the both of them could easily take on the six bandits. But, she was out cold, and the bandit leader just rounded the corner of the house, seeing Haran trying to wake Lyra up. "THE BOY, HE'S HERE," the leader shouted and the other bandits came running to his side. Haran stood, ready to face the bandits… luckily, three knives came spinning from the woods beside him, striking the first three bandits in the hearts. Orion had arrived. Haran dove into action, using the sword to parry a blow from an axe, and he jumped to the side of an attack from a cudgel. He threw his weight into an overhead sword stroke at the bandit with the cudgel who attempted to parry it. Unluckily for him, the wood from which the cudgel was made was soft and easily shattered under Haran's blow, killing him instantly. Another knife came from the woods beside Haran, striking the bandit leader in the leg. While Haran drove his sword down on the bandit with the axe, mortally wounding him. Haran looked around, and when he saw that everyone was either dead or wounded, ran to Lyra who was now awake. Orion revealed himself and walked over to the bandit leader, "How did you get out?" he asked menacingly.

"I Got a little help from a higher power," the bandit leader replied laughing.

"Well lets get you back to where you came from before I hurt you too bad," Orion said as he grabbed the wounded bandit leader and put him on Nova. Taking him back to the Norhall prison where Orion would ask to have extra cover on him.

By the time Orion got back it was dusk, Haran and Lyra had found their weapons and buried the dead bodies in the woods. "What did you find at Calcore? Any secret passages, hidden doors, or anything that would signify where that strange group went," Lyra asked as Orion walked through the door.

"Never got the chance to go, I doubled back once I saw the bandits approaching the woods," Orion said.

"So, what do we do now," Haran asked, looking to his master for an answer.

"I hate to say it," Orion said, "But we have to wait a week until we can report to the King and the Outryder commander."

Chapter 18

Before he took his new friend home the next day, Lottie had to get some food for the small creature. To feed him, he knew not to use cow milk because, as Gilpin told him the night before, "Cow's milk they can't handle, but goat's, that's what you're going to be feeding them."

So he went to get some goat's milk, the only problem, was that the closest farmer that had goats was two kilometers away, and he did not know how long the little one could live from no food. He picked up the pace, reaching the farm by early light.

On the outside of the house was a small stable for horses, and a pin for the goats, but where they got most of their money presumably was from the crop itself. Long rows of perfectly lined out crops of wheat that swayed in the morning breeze, that would bring them a pretty penny at the market in town.

The house itself was not that big, enough for two people, but no more than that to live comfortably. There was a brown and white pointer dog on the front porch, and even though he looked nice, Lottie knew that if he got close enough the dog would not be afraid to attack. Good thing he did not have to deal with that problem, because the farmer walked out of the door when he got off Midnight.

"YOU NEED SOMETHING," the farmer yelled from his porch, he didn't necessarily trust the armed warrior on his doorstep.

"I need some of your finest goats milk sir, I will pay," Lottie said, he had gotten a quite surmisable fund from the bandits raid two months ago, even if it was split between the four children, and he still had most of the money from when he won the tournament.

The farmer stepped down from the porch and approached Lottie, "How much do you need."

Lottie pulled out the tiny wolf from a satchel on Midnight's saddle, "How much do I need to feed him for two weeks, after that he will be old enough for small scraps."

The farmer examined the wolf, and after about a minute of thinking, he said, "Ok, I will get you enough, but it will cost about twenty silver." He drove a hard bargain, but Lottie knew he needed this milk now or the wolf was likely to die.

"Deal," he said, and the farmer went back inside to his supplies he was going to sell at the market.

"Here you are," the farmer said handing the milk to Lottie, "He sure is a pretty little thing aint he."

"Sure is," Lottie replied as he fed the creature, "Sure is."

Lottie got back to the Battleschool at noon, where Ella greeted him at the door. "Hey Lottie, did you get the milk?" Lottie opened his satchel full of the milk and the sleeping wolf; it had been a long night.

"Sure did, had to shell out some silvers though," Lottie replied, shaking his now lighter purse.

"It is to be expected, anyway, Heide is pretty nice, isn't she?" she asked rhetorically.

"Yeah, I guess. Are you okay?" he asked, she had never acted this perky before, and he knew something was definitely wrong here.

"Yeah fine," she said smiling…then she broke, "No I am not okay, you and Heide seemed really close last night, and I was just making sure there wasn't anything there that I should worry about."

"Really, Ella, I never picked you for the jealous type," he said jokingly, but when he saw the expression on her face, he changed tact. "No Ella, you don't have to worry about me and Heide, I like you, and your stupid little squirrel of a face."

Ella smiled, he had never openly admitted that he liked her before, even if he insulted her afterward. She had been a little worried about Heide, she was just so beautiful, and they had grown up together, and she really did not want to lose Lottie.

"Lottie, Ella," It was Battlemaster Gilpin that saw them as he had come back from the practice fields. When all the apprentices were at lunch was when he could really practice, other than when he was training with Lottie of course.

They both waved their hello's and joined their master. "Listen children, you both have to meet me at the holding dungeons at the back of the Battleschool tonight, and Lottie bring the wolf," he said as if he were just having a normal conversation. They nodded their acknowledgment, they had snuck out many times before, and figured he would be teaching them another lesson in the dungeons just as he had in the canyon.

Midnight came fast, after personal training and their dinner, they got only three hours of sleep each, until Lottie forced himself awake. He shook Ella awake and they snuck out to of the dorm room. The dungeons were at the very back of the Battleschool, meaning they needed to sneak past all the guards around the Battleschool.

It wouldn't be that hard Lottie thought, the people on watch would be fatigued from their day of training, so they would be very tired at this point in their watch. They snuck by the first person very easily, then the next and the next and the next. There was only one more guard left, a year four boy who was highly active and energized. He was about to become a knight in a month, and he really wanted to impress people with his diligence.

As Lottie tried to sneak past, he stepped on a small twig, the boy immediately swung around, "Who's there," he said in the dead of night, shining his torch over to the noise.

"Sorry, Ryan, my friend and I were just going to the dungeons to get a water jug for Battlemaster Gilpin," most of the stored water was down there so it made sense as an excuse.

He looked at them suspiciously, there was no need for a water jug in the middle of the night, and Battlemaster Gilpin would never delegate such a task that would get him fresh air. Just as he was about the signal the nearest guard however, Lottie heard a voice from behind him, "Ah there you are Lottie and El, how have you not returned yet?" it was Battlemaster Gilpin.

Ryan immediately stopped, he almost made a huge mistake, so he just shut his mouth and let them continue onto the dungeons. "Whew that was a close one," Lottie said as he followed Gilpin down the dungeon stairs.

Chapter 19

❈

The dungeons were bleak and lifeless, there was no one in there as usual, they were only holding cells after all. There were four cells, on either side of the hallway entrance, with one open wall at the end of the small hallway, where they held all their water jugs, and grains.

That's where Gilpin went to now, when he reached the end of the straight hall, he moved all the jugs out of the way so as to see the wall. Lottie was very confused at what he was doing, especially when he was feeling the wall as if he were looking for something.

He found it, at least Lottie assumed he did because he stopped at a small hole about chest level and stuck his finger in it. After about three seconds Lottie heard rocks sliding past each other, and when he turned around, he saw that the back wall of the cell to their left was not there anymore.

"What just happened," he asked confused at how his master just did that.

"Oh, Lottie boy, you have got a lot to learn about this fief," Gilpin said as he grabbed a torch of the wall, walked through the open cell door, and onto the once seal passageway. He did the same thing to the other wall and the wall went up behind him.

Lottie hated cramped spaces, and this was one of them, barely tall enough for him to stand upright, and barely wide enough to fit his large frame, this tunnel was the epitome of why. With Ella behind him and Gilpin in front, really did not help that feeling, he preferred large, open area for grass, and sunlight.

He still had his wolf friend in the satchel he had taken from Midnight, and he was sound asleep in the comfortable space. Lottie looked up to realize that the tunnel was sloping down as they were walking, "Where are we going anyway Gilpin?"

"Lottie, how much do you know about the people that lived here before Anjagor took over," Gilpin said.

"Nothing much, other than they were barbarians who repeatedly attacked us until we finally had to take over their land," Lottie replied, wondering the corollary between the two things.

"That's what the king would like you to think, truthfully, the people that were here before Anjagor were a nation of ancient builders called the Lupens, cast from society of their homes in Athons due to their worshipping of a proclaimed false god. They were a proud people; their very intelligence was halted only by their resources and creativity. They were this way for many of generations until Anjagor struck; Anjagor was relatively small at the time, with only about three fiefs to its name, but it had a military strength that was unheard of at the time. The Lupens and the Anjagorians fought hard for an entire decade with the Lupens having the upper hand, until one man, Outin Ryder, stopped it all, he almost single handedly changed the tide of the war. He was a ruthless man, killing innocent women in children in his rampage across the country, the Lupens knew that they could win the war, but at a cost. Many more women and children would have been slaughtered by the time they would have won, so they took to the underground, making secret passages and tunnels, like the one we are in right now. After the Anjagorians realized that the Lupens had just disappeared, they claimed their land as if they had won the war, and Outin Ryder was given much praise and status, they even gave him a whole division of military. The Outryders they were called, and no one ever saw the Lupens again." Battlemaster Gilpin said finally, ending his speech.

"Wow, where do you think the Lupens are now," Lottie asked.

"That's what I'm about to show you." Gilpin responded as they kept heading down in the tunnel; it would be another hour, or maybe two before they got where they were headed. A seemingly endless dark tunnel until Gilpin made a sharp right turn revealing light, and their destination.

As they entered the placed that sourced the light, Lottie was amazed, a gigantic underground civilization was in front of his eyes, and right under Norhall's nose. The ceiling was about two hundred meters above his head, with hundreds of houses built into the side walls, little springs shot up from the ground, causing a sizable river to flow through the cavern leading to a pond that filled the bottom parts of the cavern. Beside this pond, there were rows and rows of crop fields, wheat, oats, beans, rye, anything available to them, they had here. Rows of building, all organized on a slant that led up to a gigantic house at the top, three stories of the finest woods and stones that he had ever seen.

It was simply breathtaking all the lights everywhere to light up the would-be dark cave, it looked like thousands of tiny fireflies were just milling their way through a box of darkness. By the sheer amount of houses he saw, Lottie knew he wasn't looking at the population of a single fief, he was looking at the population of a small nation. A guard was posted at the entrance to the cavern, but he recognized Gilpin from his last visits and let him pass without issue.

Even though it was late into the night at this point, as they were walking down the streets, Lottie realized, that none of the lights were out. "Why are the lights still on if everyone is asleep," he asked, of all the questions, this one he asked.

"Well son, all of this light that you see in Randint Cavern actually come from light producing crystal, mined when they were still building this place, that is why the walls and the ceiling are both lit up as well as every other place in the cavern, to combat this, the residents built their windows with shutters that they close when they go to sleep."

As the three of them made their way up the sloped path to the mansion at the top, both Lottie and Ella were looking around amazed at how an entire civilization could be living under their very noses since before they were even born.

"So, this has been here all along, why are they still in hiding," Ella said.

"Yes, they have, and they are still in hiding until they have the right moment to take back their land, either by peace or by force," Gilpin replied.

"How did you come to know this place, and why do you know so much about this place," Lottie asked.

"Well, you see, the Lupens have many of their citizens all around Norhall, and Anjagor to collect intel, I am one of those citizens. A spy, they call it. I found this place twenty years ago, and I sympathized with their cause, so I joined it, and now I am one of Doran's closest advisors and friend."

"Doran? who's he," Lottie asked.

"Looks like your about to find out," Gilpin said as they approached the very extravagant door to the beautiful mansion.

Tap-Tap-Tap, went the metal ring on the door handle.

Tap-Tap-Tap

The door opened three seconds later, a small boy around eight years of age appeared in its wake. "Hey little Keryn," Gilpin said as he embraced the small child, lifting him off his feet, "How you been bud."

"Good, my daddy just taught me how to use a sword," the little boy said as he mimicked the basic sword strokes.

"That's cool bud, going to be killing them thieving bastard before you know it," he said as he set the boy down, "Speaking of bastards, where's your dad at?" Lottie stifled his laughter and Ella stomped on his foot, signaling for him to stop.

"He's in his study, but don't tell him I'm awake, if he wakes up mom, we are all in for a good spanking," Keryn said as he went back inside to his mock sword fighting.

The inside was just as beautiful as the outside, soaring ceiling, chandeliers, rugs, and a magnificently symmetric stairway leading to the banister of the second floor. How anyone could afford such a brilliantly designed house was just jaw dropping to Lottie, even the practicality of using it as a defensive fort was sound, the outside was made of different stones as not to burn, small windows at the bottom floor with no other entrance other than the main door which could be sealed by a long wooden bar, the only way to the upper floors was a gigantic staircase that could be easily defended from all sides, this place wasn't just a house, it was also a stronghold.

Tap-Tap-Tap, on Doran's study door, "Come in," a voice came from the study. So, the three entered, it was a basic study, shelves of books, a desk, and a wooden chair. Doran was standing at the window looking outside at the tiny civilization he had helped to build for the last twenty-five years.

He turned at the footsteps at the door, "Why hello my old friend," he said as he shook Gilpin's hand, "Who do you have here." Doran was a well-built man in his late forties, he had brown hair, was square jawed, and had very magnificent looking grey eyes. He also had a long scar down his cheek, a sign of a warrior, and a good one by the way he carried himself.

"My apprentices, Ella, and Lottie, I came so soon because I have a proposal…" Gilpin replied pointing to each one, respectively.

Doran shook both of their hands, and then addressed Gilpin, "We can talk logistics tomorrow for now, you three need to get your rest."

Chapter 20

Lottie woke up, had an amazing breakfast of eggs, bacon, and buttered bread, and went outside to explore the city. The streets were bustling at this time, had to be almost a thousand people going to their jobs, or to the marketplace to get their dinner for the night. Gilpin told him that he shouldn't be privy to the boring logistics of technically being a spy, and he was okay with that. Plus, at breakfast, Doran told Lottie the location of the Lupen military, which was obviously hidden so no outsider could see their ongoings.

Tap-Tap-Tap, on the study door again, "Come in," the voice came again, this time without the children. Doran wanted talk to his trusted advisor without letting the children know too much about the secrets going on in Randint Cavern.

"Gilpin, good it's you, I trust you had a comfortable sleep last night," he said, already knowing the answer.

"I did indeed, you have the finest of sheets in all of Anjagor," Gilpin replied, it was probably true he thought, they were silky and smooth, far better than his at the Battleschool.

"Fantastic, wouldn't want it any other way for my old friend," Doran said, Gilpin was the leader of his spy operation, and he trusted him with his life.

"So, why did you call me here, I am sorry about the kids by the way, I just figured we could loop them in," Gilpin said, realizing he cared deeply for them.

"Oh, that's not a problem, the more the fighters we have the better, because I think it is almost the time to take back our land," Doran said, looking out the window amongst his ardent supporters.

"Why now, what's happened," Gilpin asked, wondering what changed his friend's mind.

"Do you know why my ancestors had to move out of Athon, and into the Norhall area?"

"Yes, you told me, they worshipped a god, and were exiled by the Athons, leaving them to form another nation here," Gilpin said, wondering if it were a trick question.

"Not just any 'god', but it was *Albalupius* or commonly known as the god of destruction and revenge, the white wolf. But he was no random god at all, he was the only god that had ever descended onto the mortal plane, in fact that is what made the Lupens first start believing in *Albalupius*, did you know that?" Doran said.

"I don't suppose I did, what makes you bring it up now though," Gilpin replied after pondering his response for a short time.

"Well, you see, there is a prophecy, written by the person who founded this place a hundred years ago, would you like to see," Doran said as he opened the book on his desk to page eighty-one, the prophecy read:

Tale discovered much to late
to turn the tables or change the fate....

He finished the prophecy that was read by Orion just two weeks ago.

"Wow, it looks as if we win in the end, why do you look upset," Gilpin said looking confused by his friend's facial expression.

"Because the savior was born, two days ago, and he was taken before we could get there," Doran replied, slamming his fist against his wooden desk.

"Wait, wait, wait, how do you know? This 'savior' could have happened at any time the past or in the future," Gilpin asked, wondering why Doran was so angry.

"That is what I thought until I saw this, follow me," Doran said leading him out of the study and up to the third floor, they turned into an empty room with only a small coffin in it, and in the coffin, was Gai. Gilpin looked visibly shocked.

"I know who has the wolf, and I am really glad I decided to bring him down here," Gilpin said as he looked into the coffin and saw the bloodstained wolf in front of his eyes.

Lottie approached the fighting area, three separate pits of sand, each one about five meters in diameter, six of warriors were training on one, four more on another, and two on the final one. They were paired off sparing with their respective weapons, a battleaxe, sword and shield, voulges, spears and more. Lottie decided that he would challenge the one that looked the best, no need wasting time on the average.

There was a clear superior when he watched, a brown headed young man in his early twenties with long, well-kept hair in a low man bun. He was a little shorter than Lottie and a few years older. He was very quick and precise with his spear and buckler, landing every shot exactly where he wanted it, easily controlling his opponents every movement.

As they finished sparring, Lottie approached the young man, "Hi my name is Lottie, do you mind trying your luck with me," he said unsheathing his swords, directing the attention onto himself.

"Are you insane, Tomas would kill you if he faced you," his sparring partner said scoffingly.

"How about we just find out how good he really is," Tomas said, anyone that came in that confident was either a dangerous man or a fool, and he didn't take this young man as a fool.

They got into their fighting positions, and they began circling each one looking for a weakness in their respective opponent. Tomas thrust his spear which was easily parried, and they circled and circled. Lottie knew he needed to earn

Tomas's respect, so he began the process, side-cut, underhand, overhand, each one bouncing of Tomas's shield and onto the next. Now it was Tomas's turn, thrust, thrust each one deflected by the flick of a wrist. Then, something sparked between the two, they had a feel for each other now and went all out in a flash of excellent skill, thrust were being blocked, side-cuts were being parried everything working together in a thirty second game of chess that lasted two minutes in Lottie's head.

Even though Tomas was highly skilled, it was clear who would eventually win, Tomas was already being forced on the back foot, while Lottie pressed into his opponent. Tomas had faced many tough opponents before, but this man in front of him was not like anything he had ever seen, totally in his element as if he were a wild beast hunting a gazelle, not just any wild beast, the king of them.

In only a matter of a minute, Lottie had destroyed such a skilled opponent and held his sword at Tomas's neck as a sign for him to surrender, and he did. Lottie helped him up, he was still shocked as he realized what had just happened, he was one of the top ten best fighters in the Lupen military, and he has just been beaten convincingly by a man he had never seen before.

"Wh... Wh... Who... are you" he said stuttering from shock.

"Lottie," Gilpin's voice rang behind Lottie, "let's go, Doran and I have to show you something." Lottie grabbed his satchel off the ground and went with his master up the slopped path towards the mansion at the top.

He knew that Ella went to the markets to look for some new clothes, but apparently, she had made her way back, because she was sitting on the front porch when they approached. They nodded to each other as she got up, they would discuss what happened later, for now, Gilpin seemed serious, and that is never a good sign. They made their way to the door, and up to the third floor, where they saw Doran. Gilpin led them into the empty room where he lifted the head off the coffin.

Lottie took a shuttered breath as he saw the dead creature, his favorite in the world, "How did you get her here, and why would you show me this."

"Lottie, I know this a confusing experience, but you need to let me see your wolf cub," Doran said, "I just need to make sure he is the right one." Lottie was confused, but opened his satchel, took out his little wolf friend, who had been in there and showed it to Doran.

"Ahh yes," he said, as the white wolf was handed to him. "The savior born a wolf of white."

"What is going on Gilpin," Lottie said as he took back his little friend.

"Lottie, Ella, why don't we go eat lunch, and I will explain everything," Gilpin said.

There was a knock on the door, TAP-TAP-TAP, "Who is it," Doran asked.

"It's me darling," the voice came back.

"Oh, come in Sylvia,"

A middle-aged woman came through the door, quite beautiful for her age. Tall, blonde, and graceful as she walked in, "I just wanted to say that lunch is re…" She stopped as she made eye contact with Ella, "El? she said.

"MOM?" Ella asked.

Chapter 21

❈

Haran packed up enough clothes for a week's travel to the capital, two days travel there, three days stay, and two more days of traveling back. Orion had his monthly report to the Outryder Commander as well as the King, and he hoped to ask for advice on what to do. Haran and Lyra were coming because he did not trust to leave them alone with the amount of stuff that is going on right now. Orion had told Haran and Lyra to leave their pets at home, Shiva had gotten too big for the satchel, and he did not want Scarlett following as she usually did. Especially with not having a place to store her when they got to the castle.

They reached the border of the Anjagor and Norhall fiefs; this time no bandits to attack them, or at least none yet. They had been riding quite hard all day, and they only had about a hour of sunlight left, so they decided to stop for the night. They set up camp for the night in a small clearing about thirty meters off of the road; Lyra set up camp while Haran and Orion went to collect firewood, they really didn't say much, they had already been briefed on what they knew so far, which wasn't much, so there really wasn't much to talk about. Lyra and Haran had light conversations, but that was about it, there were no time for jokes now, this was serious.

When they got the fire started, and after they ate their dinner, there was only about thirty minutes left of daylight, Orion got up, grabbed his axes, and said, "Haran, Lyra, seeing as we might be on the brink of a war, I think it might be appropriate to share with both of you a secret move, that only myself and one of my closest friends, and former master knows. Haran come here will you."

Confused, Haran grabbed his weapons and joined Orion in the middle of the clearing. "You two are exceptionally good fighters, but let's say you find someone more skilled than you, stronger, faster, bigger. How would you go about beating them?" Orion asked, looking for input from Haran.

Haran shrugged, he had not come across this problem yet, everyone he had faced, he had easily dispatched them. "Why is it, that the Outryders uses two axes as their main weapon," Haran shrugged and Orion continued, "they have less range then swords, and if we just used one, we could carry a shield in the other. It just seems so counterintuitive to use such inferior tactics, if we wanted the best possible option as weapons, so I ask again, why we use them."

Lyra interjected, "Axes, can hook other weapons or shields, and in Outryder terms, it could be pretty advantageous, especially if wanting to disarm them without too much time or effort."

"That is true, but why would we use two smaller ones, instead of one big one, or one small one and one shield?"

Lyra shrugged, she had not thought of that, she just used them how she was taught to.

"Shields are big, and not suited for the silent way of life for an Outryder, same with a giant axe, they aren't practical while traveling silently through a forest, you would get caught of branches and vines," Orion said, but everyone in the Outryders knew these things.

"So, what's the big secret," Haran asked, noting that Orion had not really showed them it yet.

"Force…to beat an opponent stronger and faster than you, you need to use their force against them," Orion said, "And two axes as well as being the only real practical thing for the Outryder lifestyle, they are also the most practical thing for using the opponents force against them."

111

"How do you do it then," Haran asked, not understanding how they were better than shields for redirecting an opponent's force.

"Let me show you, strike me, with all your might and speed," Orion said, Haran knew that he would stop it so he sent a downward stroke with all his might at his master's skull.

Orion met it with his off-hand axe, stopping the blow dead in its tracks. Then, he put his dominant hand axe behind Haran's axe, pulling it, at the same time as pushing the off-hand axe, which sent Haran's axe back onto itself. Orion stopped it an inch in front of Haran's nose, he had rendered his opponent utterly useless in one swift movement.

Haran, disorientated asked, "How…did you do that?"

"Why don't I show you a little slower this time."

Again, downward stroke, but this time it was slow. Orion met it, then stopped, "Step one stop the opponent's weapon with your off-hand."

"Next put the dominant handed axe behind and near the base of the opponent's weapon," he continued as he performed the moves he was saying as he was doing them.

"Finally, push the dominant handed axe forward, while you pull the off-handed axe back, and it will send the opponents wrist in a frensy, trying to keep up with your irregular movement," Orion said as he sent Haran's wrist back, making him force his own axe upon himself.

"Wow, that is brilliant Orion," Lyra said.

Orion nodded his appreciation, and began working to clean up their dinner, "Why don't both of you practice it for the remainder of the day and then get some rest, because you two are going to be meeting the king tomorrow."

A looming bridge came in sight before the actual castle. Anjagor Castle was on a mountain, as most castles were, but this was different, it was a mountain where the peak, a plateau, was cut in half all the way to the bottom by a giant scar. No one knows how or when this anomaly took place, but because it is there, Anjagor Castle is almost impenetrable. The castle was a wonderful sight, towers reaching toward the sky, walls glistening off of the rising sun, flags, a combination of yellow, white, and purple hung from the crenelations.

The side of the mountain that Anjagor is on is virtually insurmountable to climb, especially when trying to take a whole army up it. Leaving the only way of sieging the castle being a giant bridge extending over a one-hundred-meter gap. The bridge itself was stone, so that it would be impossible to burn. There were two gate towers either side, and a removeable wooden piece about ten meter in length at the center of the bridge. This castle is the main reason that Anjagor was the superpower it is today. If you cannot take the capital you can't take the country, and Anjagor Castle was impenetrable.

The sun was just rising when they were stopped at the entrance to the bridge, "State your bui...", a young guard stuttered, seeing their distinct wear, and weapons and shifted to let them pass, Outryders were known for their positions of power, even if they didn't project it as a baron or royal family would, and they were not to be interrupted, "Pardon me Orion, I meant no offence by it," he said as he hung his head, waiting for the oncoming sly remark.

"What is your name boy," Orion said as if he cared greatly.

"Robin," the pale boy said.

"And what do your parents do," Orion asked.

"They are simple castle loggers Sir," Robin said, head still hung in shame.

"Head up Robin boy, it was a simple mistake, Haran here knows a lot about those," Orion said as he pats the young guard on the back and headed across the bridge with his two apprentices.

They continued their way down the bridge until Orion held his hand up signifying to stop at the entrance to the castle, "Oh Cassie, your big feet never do fail you do they," he said, turning around to see his former master, Outryder Commander, and closest friend.

Haran almost jumped off of Spirit when he wheeled around to look for someone, last he checked there was no one behind him, now there was an above middle-aged man in drab green. 'Cassie', as Orion had referred to him as, was slim built, like all Outryders, white haired, with a beard to match, blue eyed, and by the looks of him, extremely deadly.

"You know I hate that name Orion," he said, then he noticed the two children, "Well, I suppose you two are his new apprentices, I have heard a lot about you two, the name is Cassius, and I am the Outryder Commander."

They nodded their greetings as the two scruffy old men embrace, "Good to see you friend, it feels so long since last month," Orion said.

"I assume that has something to do with what is going on in Norhall fief right now," Cassius said. Orion sent a letter by pigeon, with the encrypted message of when he would be arriving, and a general briefing on what was happening in his fief. Not wanting to get too much out if the pigeon were to fall into enemy hands, whoever the enemy was.

"Yes, but why don't we see King Nigel first, and find a safer spot before I tell you any more about that," Orion replied simply.

"Fair enough, let's get going then," Cassius said as he gestured for the three to follow him to the palace.

They entered the great hall where they saw the many servants already milling around preparing the tables for royal family's breakfast. King Nigel has a wife named, Ruby, two young boys named Remi, and Nixen, and a daughter Haran's age named Eva. They walked up the stairs leading to the keep, the highest part of the castle, and where the royal family stayed. Quinton, the chamberlain, met them at the top of the stairs, "Right this way sir, the king is waiting in his office," he said as he led them down the hall to the last door.

TAP-TAP-TAP, Quinton wrapped on the door, "Come in," a muffled voice came from behind the solid oak door.

As they entered in the room, Haran was rather unimpressed, he was expecting an extravagant design, with magnificent decorations, like in the great hall. Instead, all he saw was one solid wooden desk, two cushioned chairs, and a small hearth on the side wall with a small smoldering fire.

King Nigel was a rather handsome man, he was in his mid-forties, with brown hair, like most people in Anjagor, squared-jawed with a well-groomed beard, but one distinct feature that made him so handsome, was his almost pure grey eyes.

"Ahh Cassius and Orion, two of my favorite people," Nigel said, then he saw Haran and Lyra, "And who have we here?"

"Haran, and Lyra, my apprentices," Orion replied evenly, the last meeting he had with the king, he had mentioned them briefly.

"Nice to meet you both, please Orion, Cassius, take a seat," Nigel said, and they sat, leaving the children to stand behind them.

"I hope you don't mind Nigel, but can we keep the kids in here while we talk, they can have very valid input," Orion said, he and Nigel were very close, and Orion knew that he hated being referred as 'Your Majesty', so when he could avoid it, he calls the king by his name.

"That is perfectly alright, they will need to do this at some point, might as well learn now," Nigel said, he knows that he is going to have to get to know these kids eventually if they were to become full-fledged Outryders one day, "So, what seems to be a point of concern in Norhall fief over the past months."

"Ahh yes, let me start when we were attacked by bandits..." Orion said, telling both Nigel and Cassius everything that had happened over the last few months since the bandit attack. The mysterious insignia and weird wolf pelt the bandits wore, the fake bandits, and how they were presumably set free by some mysterious figure or figures. The strange prophecy, and how it might relate to the Battlemaster of Norhall fief, and the strange cult like group that Haran saw in Calcore Canyon.

"Wow, quite the eventful few months you've had there," Nigel said.

"Yes, it has been, and I didn't want to tell Baron Ligate because I didn't know who I could trust," Orion said, he liked Ligate, but the only people he trusted with his life were in this room.

"Good call, he was a good general, but any good person can be tainted, by money or power," Nigel responds.

"To true, do you have the prophecy here? It would be a good thing to look at to see what we are dealing with," Cassius interjected.

Orion shook his head, he knew he was forgetting to pack something. "No worries," Haran said, seeing his master's face, "I have it memorized by heart," it seems all those times reading it looking for any way to change it actually came in handy, he thought to himself.

"Tale discovered much to late..." he began as the others looked at him expectantly.

Orion got out a piece of paper and wrote what was being said, as to not make Haran repeat it again and again, and handed it to Cassius, "Good work son," he said, making Haran smile a little bit.

"Seems to me, that we are dealing with a cult that worships some type of wolf god, under Calcore Canyon," Orion said as

Cassius read the prophecy, and thought back to the information provided.

"Sounds like it to me," Cassius said, "Sir," he said to the king, asking him his opinion, he had gone rather quite recently.

Nigel simply sighed, "Yeah, I've known for over twenty-five years."

Chapter 22

❖

Orion rose from his chair as he heard the words, "You have what," he yelled furiously at his king. He had been the Outryder of Norhall fief for twenty years, and the king had said nothing about a possible insurrection force under his nose.

"Relax Orion, I am sure he has a valid explanation from hiding a secret cult from us for twenty-five years," Cassius said, his own form of anger shown through his sarcasm.

"I actually do, see around the time when Anjagor was founded, the residents of what is now called the Norhall fief, were called The Lupens. They were a thriving nation, but they had loose ideals due to their worshipping of a wolf god called *Albalupius*. They had been kicked out of Athon because of the fear that their tendency for violence would lead to the demise of Athon. That fear was rightfully founded as it turned out; the Lupens ran rampage on the seed that was Anjagor at the time. And the people that they didn't kill were converted to the Lupen way, so your founder, Outin Ryder, and my grandfather stopped it," Nigel said, finally taking a breath.

"What does any of that have to do with you not telling us about it," Orion said.

"I was getting there," he said, only a little annoyed by one of his closest friends. "Ok so where was I, ah yes, after Anjagor and Outin Ryder defeated the Lupens, we sent then underground and they agreed never to show their faces again. I am so sorry, but I assumed the group would never come out of hiding. However, Doran, apparently, has heard about the prophecy, and figured this would be the time to reclaim their lands."

"Doran, who is that?" Lyra asked.

"The leader of the Lupens, and someone who has been a pain in my side seemingly since he was born," Nigel responded. Orion were confused by the phrasing but decided to move on.

"Well, we will talk about hiding important information from an advisor later, but for now what do we do?" Cassius asked.

"For now, we wait until they formally act," Nigel said. There was an uproar from Orion and the two apprentices, they had been waiting long enough, and they were through with it.

"Listen, Listen, Listen, we cannot, and I repeat, cannot, attack without provocation, if this were to happen, we might have another type of war on our hands, the civil kind." Orion knew the king was right, but he still didn't like the idea of a secret cult under his nose.

Orion told Haran and Lyra they were no longer needed so could talk to the King and Cassius alone. After they walked out of the door, Orion looked at two of his closest friends, knowing there was only one way to get information about the Lupens' operations. "Are you two thinking what I am thinking?" he asked.

"It would be a gamble, and it might well get them killed Orion," Cassius said.

"They are my apprentices Cassius, I know what their capabilities are," Orion responded.

"Just do whatever you need to do to stop this mess," Nigel said finally.

Orion nodded and was about to continue to the next topic until he remembered something, "Oh yeah one more thing, there is a young bridge guard named Robin, make him a captain, he is a leader of men that one is." Nigel wrote the name down, and they continued on to the specifics of Orion's plan.

Haran thought they might need a little practice, so he went with Lyra to the practice arena. It was basic arena beside the barracks for the garrison for the castle; it was a ten-meter by ten-meter square with a sand floor. There was no one there, most would be at breakfast, the others on guard.

"Want to go?" Haran asked smiling at the beautifully rugged girl in front of him. Her hair was pulled back in a ponytail as opposed to the usual way where it was flowing down past her shoulders.

"Want to lose?" She replied, she knew that Haran was better, but she would never admit it.

"Fair enough, how about we practice Orion's technique," he replied, he did not want to fight with their real weapons anyway. They had only practiced the move Orion had taught them last night for thirty minutes or so, and that was slim in comparison to the amount of practice that an Outryder practices every day.

"We should come up with another name for it, what are you thinking," Lyra asked, after all she did not want to keep calling it 'Orion's technique'.

"How about Contrium," Haran said, recalling his class on the ancient language.

"What does that mean," Lyra asked, unfamiliar with the word.

"Reversal," Haran replied. She nodded, she had to admit, it had a ring to it.

"Ok then, lets practice Contrium," Lyra replied, as she unsheathed her axes.

And they did, for three hours, Block, Behind, Push, Pull. Block, Behind, Push, Pull. Block, Behind, Push, Pull.

Garrison guards cycled through after eating their lunch, and seemingly confused by the technique one said, "Why don't you try it against a sword."

"Fine by me, need some experience against swords anyway," Haran said, leaving Lyra to gracefully step aside.

Before they began the guard said, "And this move works on every angle?"

"Yes," Haran said instantly.

At that instant, the guard leapt forward with his longsword, trying to catch Haran off guard. Of course it didn't work however, Haran was far to fast for a surprise attack of that nature. Blow after blow, Haran easily brushed off, looking for the perfect opportunity to use the move.

And he found it, he had realized that when the guard was striking, he was focusing on Haran's off-hand, subconsciously waiting him to perform the move. Knowing this, Haran switched it up, stopping a side stroke with his dominant hand, and sticking his offhand behind the longsword. Pushing and pulling he sent the sword airborne, burying it deep into the sand when it fell.

"Good work young man, you're a real natural," the guard said as he went for a handshake.

"Thank you, sir," Haran said, completely unaware of the two figures in the shadows across the courtyard.

The two figures looked on in awe at the young apprentice, "The boy learns fast," Cassius said.

"Yes, takes after his father in that regard," Orion replied.

"Yes, he does, and he is going to need it because what we are about to face is unlike anything he has ever seen before; he needs to be ready," Cassius said, they were preparing for a war, and he knew that Haran would be pivotal to it.

"He will be," Orion said, looking over at his young apprentice, the prophecy running through his mind:

Two sons battle on a canyon's edge.
Where the final blow will drive the wedge.

He knew Haran was the sons in the prophecy, if so, if anything happened to him, nobody but himself could be to blame.

Chapter 23

❖

"MOM!?!?!?," Ella responded as she went to embrace her mother.

"Mom? You two are related," Doran said, just as confused as Lottie and Gilpin.

After they broke their embrace, Sylvia turned around and said, "Yes, I have got a lot of explaining to do, to both of you. Come along, might as well do it over breakfast."

Six chairs were sat around a large circular table, Keryn, Doran's son, had already finished eating, and was cleaning up his plate. As they entered, he swiftly exited to practice swordplay. They all sat, eggs, fish, ale, bread, and cheese lined the table. It was a basic breakfast, but it was an amazing one.

They all looked around awkwardly, waiting for someone to say anything, "Ok mom, why don't you start from the beginning."

"Fair enough," she said, "Well, as you know, I met your dad in Blackrock village in Osmole fief in a tavern that I worked in, we hit it off, got married, and had you. We moved to Osmole village because of the protection of the castle; that was where we made the first mistake. When you were around six, the Athons came, raiding Osmole village, we tried to make it to the castle, but we knew we were not going to make it in time. That is when you father picked up a sword of the ground and fought off the Athons, giving me and you time to get in the castle."

"Yes mom, I was there, but how did you end up here," Ella said, as she tried not to replay her father's gruesome killing in her head.

"I am getting there, I was telling that part for him," Sylvia said as she pointed to her new husband.

"Anyway, after your father's death, I was heartbroken to even look at you, everything you did reminded me of him. So, I asked your grandfather if he knew where I could go to escape from the pain that I felt, and he recommended I come here, to join the Lupens. And that is when I met the charming Doran and made a new life with him."

She finally finished, she was happy with Doran, and that was evident; however, that did not stop Ella from being upset. Her mother had abandoned her, and she had felt the same pain from her father dying, "You had no excuse to abandon me; how do you think I felt, to have my mother abandon me right after my father died?"

"I know darling, and I am sorry, and I regret making that decision, but I want you to know, it was not your fault, it was mine, and I am very sorry for making yo go through that," Sylvia said genuinely.

"We will discuss this later, for now," Ella said to her mom, then she turned to Doran, "Explain why you took so much interest in Lottie's wolf, and what is this prophecy you are talking about."

A deep sigh came from the man, and a slight glance towards Gilpin, Gilpin nodded, giving Doran the go ahead. He explained everything, the prophecy, the Lupens, the 'savior', and when he plans to take back Norhall fief.

When he finished, a litany of questions was running through both of the children's heads, but they did not ask any. The three adults were looking at Lottie for approval; Doran offered a hand, and Lottie shook it. Like it or not, he was a part of this now, and he liked it.

"And what of the wolf, what shall we call him," Doran asked.

Lottie realizing that he had the choice said, "How about Lupe."

"Now the one thing about this wolf, is that it will grow bigger than any wolf you have ever seen, and you will be expected to be able to control him." Doran said.

"Of course, I will practice with him everyday," Lottie said confidently.

"Ok, why don't you go get acquainted with Lupe, I have a feeling that once he listens to you, there is no stopping the takeover," Gilpin said.

In the dead of night, Gilpin entered the study, "You wanted to see me sir," Gilpin said.

"Yes, close the door," Doran said, Gilpin complied, "You tell me there is a rival to your apprentice?"

"Yes, Orion's apprentice, Haran, he and Lottie were at each other's throats during a tournament and when we raided that bandit camp," Gilpin said, "Oh, and by the way, was that you who sent the first bandits after them?"

"Yes, Orion has been a thorn in my side, so I tried to eliminate him as quick as possible, seems as though you can't kill an Outryder that easy," Doran said, scoffing at his blatant mistake, "Will the boy be a problem for Lottie?"

"Lottie is a natural, but so is Haran, it would be close, but if Lottie were to fight hard, he would gain the upper hand," Gilpin said.

"If...Ifs and buts do not win wars, and IF I cannot count on Lottie to win. I will have to take it into my own hands," Doran said.

Gilpin immediately knew what he was talking about, "Do you really want to do it?"

"I have bent my knees to him long enough, I think it's time I show him that I have what it takes," Doran said, looking up towards the ceiling, as if he were looking someone through the tons of rocks above his head.

Chapter 24

❊

"SHIVA, SHIVAAA, WHERE DID YOU GET OFF TO," Haran shouted as he walked through Fuestres Woods. Shiva seemed to have a mind of her own these days, running off every time she saw a hare or squirrel, and not coming back for several hours at a time. She had grown even bigger, and now she thought she was in charge.

"You need to train her, the reason she keeps running off like that is because you haven't given her a reason to stay here," Orion said, and even though it came off harsh, Haran knew he was right.

"I know, and I am going to start tomorrow," Haran said, like he had been telling himself for the past ten days.

"As you have said, but as we all know, procrastination is the enemy of success, in this case, it is the enemy of me not hearing you scream your stupid pet's name every five seconds." Orion said.

They had gotten back from Anjagor Castle a fortnight ago, and while Orion was trying to figure out a plan to stop the Lupens, Haran and Lyra were left to train around the clock. Haran decided it would be a good thing to have a trained killer in Shiva, however he waited too long and now he had a bigger problem on his hands.

He went back to his training THUNK-THUNK-THUNK… three hours later, Shiva came back with a dead squirrel in her mouth and dropped it at Haran's feet for approval. Haran just sighed and continued with his throwing.

The next day, Haran got up earlier than usual, he had finally gotten the desire to train the creature. "Shiva," he whispered as he crept his way outside, trying not to wake anyone. Her head popped up curiously and she followed him outside.

It was a foggy morning, to the point where the only thing you could see were the slight rays of sunlight bouncing off of the thickness of the blanket of fog. He decided to start with basic commands, sit, stay, lay, follow, to do this he brought out some raw fish he had caught yesterday in the spring, she always loved to eat fish.

"Sit," Haran said as he held out a tiny piece of fish.

Smelling it, Shiva immediately became interested, she did not know what he wanted, but she at least knew he wanted something, and more importantly, that he had something to offer her. Haran bent down and patted the ground behind Shiva as she stood curiously, watching the piece of food.

"Sit girl, sit," Haran said again as he patted the ground for a second time.

Finally understanding what her master wanted from her, she planted her hind on the damp grass.

"Good girl," he said, as he gave her a piece of the fish.

After about half an hour of teaching her to sit, he decided to move on to teaching her to stay. An hour later, Orion came outside seeing the cat sitting on the ground, waiting for Haran to turn around and see him. "She learns fast huh," Orion said after a few minutes of waiting.

Haran whipped around, wondering how long he had been standing there, "Yeah, I guess she does do she."

"Remind you of someone," Orion asked Haran, who went to join him.

He thought about it for a minute then shook his head, "You Haran, well you and Lyra," Orion said, replying to his own question.

Confused, Haran decided not to respond, so Orion continued, "Do you know why I chose you and Lyra as my apprentices?"

Haran again shook his head, "It wasn't because of your skill, or your intelligence, or your ability to get on my last nerve," Haran smiled, he did tend to do that a lot, "But it was your ability to learn things, both of you, have extraordinary learning capabilities. Think about it, within five months you have learned as much as a two-year Outryder apprentice."

"Most of that was from an excellent teacher," Haran said, Orion smiled, it was a rare occurrence for the grizzled man.

"Haran, there is something I have to ask you to do for me that might put you in grave danger, Lyra is already on board," Orion said.

"What is it," Haran asked curiously, Orion did not ask for things, he either told, or did.

"I need you to get recruited to be a Lupen," Orion said skeptically waiting for Haran's response.

Haran was confused by this request, but he thought about how much Orion had done for him so he answered, "Of course."

"You don't have to do this Haran," Orion said, he was asking his apprentice to go into enemy territory with no help from his master.

"No, it's my duty to do this, especially if it could stop the prophecy before someone dies. Now, what do we have to do," Haran replied.

"Why don't we go inside, and I will brief you on everything," Orion said.

Lyra was sitting at the table skimming through papers, presumably ones on the Lupens. Haran sat down beside her and smiled, she had a bird's nest of nap growing from her hair from just waking, but it was kind of cute, Haran thought.

"Ok Haran as I explained to Lyra, what you will be doing is getting a Lupen recruiter's attention saying something about how much you hate the king or something along those lines. Once you get in there, try to learn as much as possible, about their military, their strategies, and their leader, Doran. Now, King Nigel and I think Sir Gilpin and Lottie are working hand and hand with the Lupens, so, and I mean this, you two cannot, and I repeat cannot be seen by Lottie. Reports say he disappeared for a couple days last week with Gilpin and another Battleschool student, but he has returned, so he should not be where you are going. Either way though, you two need to be on your guards, I wish I could go with you, but I am afraid I am too recognizable." Orion said finally finishing his spiel.

"When do we leave," Haran asked, ready for his new adventure.

Orion thought about that for a little bit, and finally said, "Tomorrow you will get the recruiters attention, and the day after that he will want you to meet him with all of your things, the one thing is though, you cannot take your horses, but you can take Shiva and Scarlett, if you are careful who sees them."

Haran flinched subconsciously, he had really come attached to Spirit, and being gone for an indefinite time would cause him a good deal of grief.

"I know, I know, it sucks, but you don't have to go through this," Orion said.

"No, its fine, what will our cover stories be?" Lyra asked.

Orion wavered for a second, never a good sign, "See that's the thing to sell it you have to go as a couple."

"A COUPLE," Lyra roared louder than she had ever been.

"Are you insane?" Haran asked.

"Oh, come on guys, it won't be that bad, you will be fine," Orion said, hoping this was not where he was going to lose them.

"Why not brother and sister, or just friends," Lyra asked.

"Because those two are not believable, you two don't look similar enough to be brother and sister, and if you say you are friends, a litany of question would come your way," Orion said, but he immediately knew it was a lie. In fact, they did look close enough to be brother and sister, and not many things could go wrong if they were friends; he liked seeing them together, and he would not be opposed to seeing them in an actual relationship.

Haran and Lyra were skeptical about it, but they finally gave way to the backwards logic. "Ok, fine," Haran and Lyra said finally after a quick glance to each other.

Tomorrow came quickly after hours of training and teaching Shiva tricks. Haran woke up and packed the bare essentials. Yesterday, Orion bought a small cage for Haran and Lyra each to store their pets when they were with the Lupens.

Per Cassius' information on recruiters in Norhall fief, there was one in the village, that usually hung out at the tavern below the inn most of the day. The White Tail was the only two-story building in the village, the tavern on the bottom floor, and the rooms to stay in on the top.

The sun was going down when they entered the tavern, there were two dozen people in there, all of them just getting back from long days at work and looking for a drink before they went back to their homes. Haran immediately spotted the guy they were looking for at a table in the back. As Orion described him, he was stocky with brown hair and brown eyes, a little on the chubby side, and looked as if he hadn't used the sword hung at his waist for years.

Haran, holding Lyra's hand to direct her through the bustling townsfolk, led her to a free table next to the chubby man. They made small talk for a few minutes until a bar wench came by asking what if they would like a drink. Obviously, they were in a tavern, so to sell it Haran replied with, "Of course, one for m'lady as well."

After a few more minutes, the drinks were put on the table, Haran lightly sipped lightly on his ale, trying his hardest not to retch in disgust. Lyra did the same, and began their rehearsed lines, "Oh c'mon Herald, we can move to the capital, make a new life, be protected by the castle." Herald Lightfoot was the alias given to Haran by Orion, Lyra's was Leida Lightfoot, newlyweds, born and raised in Norhall fief ready to make a family under the protection of others.

"No Leida, we have already been over this, I will not give that dreaded king Nigel any reason to tax me more," Haran replied, even though they were young, they sure acted the part very well, he thought to himself.

That seemed to peak the recruiter's interest, he turned his head slightly, and unconsciously, expecting more angst toward the king, and Anjagor in general. That is usually how he picked up people, recruits, apprehensive to king's rules or taxes, they try and make a new life with the Lupens, he didn't see these people as any different, even if they were young.

"I know, but where else are we going to find enough protection to where we don't have to worry about our future children being slaughtered by Bianet raider, or the Athons or just random bandits..." she trailed off Lyra was so unbelievably good at acting, even Haran started worrying about their future, fictional kids.

"I might be able to help you with that," the man said as he turned around to Haran and Lyra, or as he knew them Herald and Leida. A smile perked both their lips, and he had realized he had gotten their attention, "The name's Hawthorn, Ray Hawthorn."

"Hi Ray Hawthorn, what do you mean 'You might be able to help us with that,'" Haran asked.

"Well, I live in a secret place, under Norhall fief, that is big, and well protected, you could live there, we always love new people, and you look as if you can handle yourself," Ray said to Haran, he had already taken the bait, now it was time to draw them in.

"Really? Maybe we should go there Herald," Lyra said energetically.

"Ok, tell me all about it," Haran said as he leaned in to hear Ray speak.

They went through the intricacies of Randint Cavern long into the night, until they were kicked out by the Innkeeper. They stepped outside, and Haran finally said, "Yeah, of course we will stay, when and where do you want us to be all packed up and ready."

"Tomorrow morning, right in this spot, with all of your belonging," Ray said.

"We will be there," Haran said, and Lyra nodded her head.

As they each turned around and headed to their respective homes, Haran whispered to Lyra, "It's like taking candy from a baby." Lyra kept it going, "A giant one at that," leading Haran to laugh hysterically, he was going to enjoy this he thought to himself.

Chapter 25

❉

The next day, they met Ray outside The White Tail with all their things. Ray noticed the medium sized cage that they had, "Got yourselves some pets huh?"

"Yes, I hope that is fine, they won't be a problem," Haran said, hoping he shared the same consensus.

"That is totally fine, many Lupen people have pets," Ray said happily.

Haran smile and followed Ray with all his things. Ray led them to a small shack at the edge of town, Haran always thought it was a privy, but when they went in there, he realized how wrong he was. The only thing in there was a staircase leading down to a small, well lit, and sparsely decorated room. A small kitchen, a bed, and a small table with three chairs either side. A little confused Haran asked, " What is this?"

"This is Randint Cavern, its great isn't it," Ray said, a smile encroaching his face as he saw Lyra and Haran's faces.

"Yeaaaahhh," Lyra said, wondering if Orion had given them bad information.

A few minutes passed while Haran and Lyra walked around the tiny room. Haran heard a noise, some sort of laughter coming from behind him, he looked, to see Ray doubled over in sheer joy, all the fat sprawled out below him. "I got yall so good, yall actually thought..." he coughed due to his laughter, "Yall actually thought, that this was Randint Cavern."

"Yeah, because you told us that this was Randint Cavern," Lyra said frowning at what was happening.

"Ok, Ok, Ok, let me show you the real way to Randint Cavern," Ray said still laughing a little.

He walked over to the farthest wall, Haran had noticed before, a finger sized hole in the wall; Ray stuck his finger in it. The wall closest Haran mysteriously went down in front of his eyes, bewildered, he stumbled back. "Wha… What just happened."

"I don't even know how it works, just follow me through, it will be cramped with all your stuff, but we should make it," Ray said as he walked through the door. After they walked through, he stuck his finger in another hole; the rock wall went back into place.

They went through a tunnel about one and a half men wide, the tunnel was not well lit, but there was a lit torch at the entrance that Ray had grabbed before he went in. Haran memorized everything about the tunnel, as to write it down later in a personal journal. He noticed every turn, the angle of the slope downward, and how long it took for them reach the end. It was hard to tell time with no sun, but he assumed it to be a 4–5-hour trip.

It took forever for them to see the light of Randint Cavern. When they rounded the last bend, Haran and Lyra were amazed, a vast, lit cave was in front of them. They came out in the center of the slope upward, they saw a litany of tiny springs, forming a bigger river, that lead to a pond and three crop fields. There were rows of houses and building leading all the way up to the top of the hill where there was a mansion the size of a small castle.

Haran had many questions, but he thought the most likely one for his character to ask was, pointing towards the mansion, "Who lives up there?"

"That's where Doran and his family live," Ray replied as he followed the finger.

"And where will we be living," asked Lyra.

"There are many empty houses for newcomer, I will go register you two in for one," Ray said, and made his way up to the giant mansion on the top of the slope.

They decided to go exploring while waiting for Ray to return, they assumed they had about an hour for him to get to the top and back. They split two ways, Lyra going up, while Haran went down, both making mental notes along the way.

Haran followed the main street where there were many people going to and from their works or the markets. He went down a backstreet instead of having to walk through that many people. Based on the people he saw there, he assumed that in total, there would be close to thirty thousand people in Randint Cavern, and he assumed that about one in every five people would be warriors, those number are about half of those of Anjagor as a whole. He decided he need to find where they train these people, but he had run out of time, so he started heading back.

"Find anything?" Lyra asked.

"Not really, just got a rough estimate of the amount of people here, but I really need to figure out how their military is trained," Haran replied, that task had been specifically given to him by Orion, Lyra had the task of seeing how their production operated, and how they fed so many people. The two were both especially important for totally different reasons, if they knew the Lupen's military strength, they could develop a winning tactic. If they knew their means of production, maybe they could plan some type of sabotage.

"Nothing on my end either," Lyra said as she shrugged.

Before Haran could respond, he saw the pudgy man struggling his way through the crowd of people and decided to just join him. "Did you register us?" he asked as he and Lyra walked up.

"Of course, of course, here I will show you to your new dwellings," Ray said as he led them down a side alley away from the crowd. He led them to a small, basic, wooden house about three or four blocks from their current location, "Its small, but there are two rooms, a small kitchen, and a hearth in there, so not to bad for a start." Ray said.

"We will have to pay for any of this," Haran asked, he thought it was a valid question for anyone to ask, it would be to good to be true if not.

"Of course, unless you are a member of the Lupen military," Ray said.

"How do I join that," Haran asked seeing this a perfect segue into the conversation.

"You have to be native born I'm afraid," said Ray, it was a sound policy to not let immigrants into a secret rebellious force, but very annoying for Haran.

"Ah well, what can you do," Haran said trying to pass it off as a one-off comment.

"Yes well, I will let you both get acquainted to your new homes, in five days you will have a mandatory worship service for Albalupius as we discussed last night. I will be by tomorrow asking you to report to Doran for your job assignment and evaluation; I will see you then," Ray said as he walked away from the two of them.

After they got inside, they looked around, it was exactly as Ray had described it, two rooms, a small kitchen, and a hearth, nothing more nothing less. "So, what are you going to do if you can't get a spot in the military," Lyra asked, genuinely concerned for Haran.

Haran looked up with a devilish hint to his eyes, "Oh don't you worry about me; I've already got a plan."

Chapter 26

❈

Lottie was disappointed when Gilpin told him he had to leave Randint Cavern, but the one thing that cheered him up, was that they got a semester break only a week from now, and he was told he could go back then. Lottie was finding his place among the Lupens, becoming one of Doran's friends. He was also becoming a semi-famous warrior from his stunt with Tomas, who was apparently a captain in the Lupen military.

Ella had also found her place in Randint Cavern with her mother, and while Lottie had to leave, she decided to stay; she always wore a head covering around the Battleschool, and her only friend was Lottie, so no one would notice her sudden disappearance.

Lottie took Lupe with him to get acquainted with his horse, Midnight, it was weird to look at them side by side, the sheer contrast of Lupe's pure white and Midnight's jet black always gave Lottie a headache.

It was three days until the end of the semester, and Lottie was teaching Lupe tricks in Malen Plains an hour after breakfast. Clip-Clop-Clip-Clop, he heard the hoofbeats behind him, a familiar sound to him, "Lottie," Gilpin said.

Lottie turned around to look at him waiting for him to continue, "You're in luck," he said.

"Oh, how is that" Lottie asked as he called Lupe over from where he was chasing a small rabbit.

"I have got news from Baron Ligate, that there was a Bianet raiding ship spotted near the coast of Whitmer."

Whitmer was a small village in Dalhurst fief that was about 5 kilometers from Hermirtha Sea, a historically prime place for Bianet raids. "Well, what are we doing here, let's go," Lottie replied as he ran to where Midnight was, Lupe following behind. The craftsmen of Randint Cavern had made him a side piece for Midnight's saddle that easily allowed Lupe to jump into when he was going anywhere. Obviously, they couldn't have horses in Randint Cavern, but Doran still thought it was a good idea.

"So, where are we going, the Battleschool or straight there?" Lottie asked. It was protocol for them to return to the Battleschool and raise a sizeable force.

"We are going straight there, Sir Lerin is gathering three dozen of the finest students to move as soon as possible,'" Gilpin said.

"How many ships are there," Lottie asked, as he knew, many Bianet raider boats hold around thirty men.

"The scout said that there was only one, so it should be plenty enough to push back against the raid," Gilpin said.

To get to Whitmer, it would take half a day on their horses, they expected for the Bianet raider to attack at dawn the next day, so they had plenty of time.

They had been traveling for three hours when they stopped for lunch, and as they began riding again Gilpin asked, "Lottie, how do you feel about Orion's apprentice, Haran." He had noticed the tension back when they raided the bandit camp and was trying to pry it out of him.

"Ummm, me and Haran have a long history of mutual hatred, why do you ask?"

"No reason." Gilpin said, giving it about a minute, then he spoke again, "I noticed he was quite good with those axes of his, perhaps even better than you."

Lottie scoffed at the pure insanity that came out of his mentor's mouth, "Haran, ch- are you kidding, he couldn't beat me in a thousand lif…" He stopped, not wanting to sound too self-confident.

"I don't know, I think he gives you a run for your money," Gilpin said as he urged his horse to greater speeds, there was no more need to pry any further, he had already planted the seed.

They reached the small town, about three hours after noon. It was a relatively unimpressive site, a small river, a few houses, a small inn, and a small marketplace. "Why would anyone want to raid this place," Lottie asked.

"They raid this place due to its proximity to the water, but it hasn't been raided this year, so they see it as Whitmer having their resources replenished," Gilpin replied.

They made their way to down to the small village, they were there before Sir Lerin and his men, so they had to go talk to the village elders and inform them of the raid.

A young man who was maybe a year or two older than Lottie had a sword hung at his belt approached them, "Who are you, and what is your business." Gilpin felt disrespected, but he also knew that it was raiding season, and you had to be on your guard to survive.

"Battlemaster Gilpin of Norhall fief," Gilpin said, noticing the boy shift slightly and look down from embarrassment that he disrespected the knight. Gilpin thought this was a good enough as an apology, so he continued, "A Bianet raiding ship is off the coast 5 kilometers that way," Gilpin said as he pointed south towards the Hermirtha Sea.

"Oh, well yes you are welcome to stay as long as you would like, I am Walter by the way," the young man said, thinking it was rude not to introduce himself.

"Thank you, we will be staying in that field over there; there should be a few dozen more men coming, so let them know when they arrive," Gilpin said, and the boy nodded.

They set up camp in a field about one-hundred meters from Whitmer Village, just setting up a tent each, and Gilpin going into the village to tell the village elders to tell their citizens to remain inside at dawn tomorrow.

Lottie walked into the village to get fresh food for the night when the Walter approached them again, "Hello again, do you think Sir Gilpin would mind if I helped fight against the Bianets?" He had been looking for a chance to use his sword in action, Whitmer was rather calm most of the year, and maybe if the Battlemaster saw him fight he might see something him and recruit him.

"I'm sure he wouldn't mind, the more the merrier right," Lottie said, seeing the sword at Walter's belt, and assuming he had to know how to use it.

Before Walter could thank him, a rather good-looking raven headed town girl walked up behind him, "Walt, let's go."

"Sorry would love to talk, but I got to take my girl hunting, it's her first time, I am sure you understand," Walter said, Lottie just smiled as he walked away.

"Actually, I don't understand," he said sadly under his breath, he had never had a girlfriend, and he had not had time to take Ella out on a true date.

The 'reinforcements', arrived at sunset, and set up their tents in the same open field, "Battlemaster," Lerin said nodding as he entered the fairly sizeable control tent, they had set up for Gilpin, Lerin, and Lottie to discuss tactics in private.

"Sir Lerin, what are you thinking for tactics," Gilpin said. He already knew the most optimum solution to the problem at hand, but he figured he would ask as a sign of respect.

"Well, there is a spot right here," Lerin replied as he pointed to the map in front of him, "It is the narrowest part of the road, surrounded by densely packed forest that would be near impossible to get through while maintaining the element of surprise. So, I say, we ambush them here, take them by surprise instead, and surround them, allowing no escape."

Gilpin nodded his agreement, but Lottie was shaking his head, "Won't work, from what I have heard, the Bianets fight like scared dogs, surround them and they bite harder than ever. I propose we hide in the village, taking them out one by one as they split up, that will lose us less unexperienced soldiers."

Gilpin cringed as he heard Lottie correct the man, Sir Lerin was a good man but, as many with positions of authority, they tend to think they are always right. Lerin's face turned blood red with rage, "Who are you to be telling me son, you haven't even finished your first year at the Battleschool…"

Wanting to stop any future conflict, Gilpin shouted, "SHUT UP." He waited for Lerin to quiet down, then continued in a subdued voice, "We shall be at this chokepoint tomorrow an hour before dawn." He looked at Lerin then to Lottie and back at Lerin, "Copy?"

"Copy," they both said simultaneously.

Lottie went to town to tell Walter about where to meet them tomorrow and what time. He found him coming back from the woods with his girlfriend, who was named Faith, and explained the details.

"You sure you're ready," Lottie asked, sensing his nervous energy.

"Of course, born that way," Walter responded goofily as he smiled at Faith.

Chapter 27

❈

They woke up two hours before sunrise, packed up their weapons, and headed to the predesignated ambush location. The cartographer of Dalhurst fief was the best in the business, getting it down to the last little tree and rock on the road.

Walter arrived around ten minutes after they did and went over to where Lottie and Gilpin were by the road. "What's he doing here," Gilpin asked as he recognized the young man approaching.

"Oh sorry, I forgot to mention, he wanted to help against the Bianets, so I said he could join us," Lottie replied. Gilpin nodded; they always needed more hands on.

The Bianets appeared down the long stretch of road from Witmer to the Hermirtha Sea. Lottie shifted a little, he had never actually seen a Bianet raider before; he had seen drawings of course, but these people looked different from the drawings. The raiders in the drawings had large horned helmets and little clothing on, but these raiders wore bowl shaped helmets with prominent nose guards, and they had what looked like multiple layers of pelts and cloth. Big shields were slung on their backs and small axes like the ones Haran wore were at their belts.

"That them?" Lottie whispered to Gilpin. To which Gilpin simply nodded.

The raiders walked only two meters away from where Lottie was standing, by his count there were thirty-two, not more than their own numbers, but a serious amount to do damage.

As planned, Lerin stepped out in front of the raiders ten meters down the track, the raiders stopped and the man at the front, presumably the party leader called in his native language. "Common tongue please," Lerin shouted back.

Lottie could only make out one word said to as the leader gestured towards Lerin, 'Sla' which Lottie knew meant, 'Kill'.

The Bianet raiders slowly approached the man in the road, but they would never get to him because after the first couple steps they took towards him, three dozen men jumped from behind bushes and trees wreaking havoc on the unsuspecting raiders. Their numbers were cut a third by the time they even realized what was happening, Lottie, after dispatching two raiders, decided to look around for anyone who seemed to be struggling, and that person was Walter. Lottie realized he really should have tested Walter's ability with a sword before letting him in the heat of battle, the boy was swinging wildly at the trained warrior in front of him, and in a matter of seconds he would be dead.

Lottie rushed over towards where Walter was fighting. He parried the overhand blow aimed at Walter and began on the offensive. His blistering speed sent his swords into shining arcs. With the sheer speed and precision being too much for the raider to handle, Lottie's sword cut through his pelt torso and into his stomach, sending the raider wailing onto the floor.

Lottie turned around to look for Walter, "Hey, thanks for the save, maybe you could teac…" Before Lottie could even warn him, a Bianet raider came up behind Walter, shoving his sword through his liver, killing him instantly.

"NOOOOOO!" Lottie screamed across the battlefield as he saw Walter's eyes went cold, and his body hit the ground. In rage, Lottie killed the raider in one sword stroke, and looked around to see if there were any more to kill. There was half a dozen left, but they were surrendering so he took ahold of Walter's lifeless body; as he held the young man, blood running through his hands as he thought back to Walter's girlfriend, Faith, how would he tell her of what he had let happen to her boyfriend.

After Gilpin rounded up the Bianets and got them tied up, he walked over to Lottie, who had been mourning over Walter's dead body for ten minutes now. "It's not your fault son, its life," he said, but it was his fault, all he had to do was say no, or even say 'let me see what you got'. However, now there was a dead man in his arms, a dead man because of him.

"NOO!! GILPIN ITS ALL MY FAULT, I DID THIS, AND I----," Lottie choked on his tears, then stopped yelling as loud, "I will have to tell this man's girlfriend, that I let him die on my watch." After Lottie finished, he picked up the lifeless body, brushed past Gilpin, onto Midnight, and onto Faith.

Faith knew what had happened as soon as she saw the boy's face, the boy from last night, Lottie, his face was red, puffy, and full of sheer grief, "No, No No No No No, It cant be he cant be dead, he just proposed to me yesterday, he cant be dead," she kept repeating.

She ran to Lottie who was now getting off Midnight; she looked at where Walter's body was, "What happened," she asked, tears flowing down her face.

"He protected me from a Bianet raider, I was being cornered from all sides, and he got them off me enough for me to deal with the others. However, in the process a raider snuck up on him and…". Lottie hated lying, but it was for the greater good, he could not let Faith think her deceased boyfriend was incompetent, that would just break her.

"Really???" She asked as if she did not believe him.

"Yes, Walter was a great man, you should have been proud to have called him your fiancé," Lottie said wholeheartedly, he was not lying about this part.

"What do I do now? He was my life, we were going to build a life together somewhere away from this place," she asked rhetorically, she didn't expect anyone to have the answer to that question.

But someone did, Gilpin, who appeared from seemingly nowhere said, "Come with us, the place we live is beautiful, away from here, safe and secure. You could start a life there, there is plenty of room."

She raised her eyebrows, wiped off her tears, and said, "Seriously, you would do that?"

"Of course, we owe you one." Lottie replied.

Chapter 28

❈

Haran had been trying to find where the Lupen military trained for three days now to no avail. He had searched every street, and every building in Randint Cavern, "IT HAS TO BE SOMWHERE," he told Lyra the third night, he was aggravated with his lack of findings.

She had already found out about most of the means of production of Randint Cavern and was telling him to write down her findings as she said them. "Three farms, each one producing different crops. There are several leatherworkers, bakers, cobblers, weavers and only one blacksmith forge with five to seven workers in it at a time..."

Haran's head shot up, of course he thought, the blacksmith, any military needs weapons and armor, and the blacksmith would produce those weapons and armor.

"Where are you going," Lyra asked as Haran bolted outside of the door.

"BLACKSMITH," Haran shouted as he ran out into the street.

"That boy," Lyra said. He was so weird, she thought.

Haran walked into the blacksmith around midday, it was far away from any other building so that if it were to set fire it would not burn the whole city down. Also, because it was a fiery, loud setting with five people banging on anvils at the same time making several different items ranging from nails to plate armor. There was one huge forge in the direct center with several different anvils and hammers as well as several different wide tubes filled with water was to quench the pieces.

One blacksmith, who had just finished quenching a blade noticed his entrance and walked up to him. He was an older man, but was well muscled and looked healthy, "How may I serve you today young man, care for nails or some armors do you."

"No actually, just information," Haran replied.

"Ask away sonny, I just might be able to help," the man said.

"Well, I was wondering, if you knew someone I could talk to as to get a shot at becoming Lupen military," Haran asked, he had been mulling over this question for a long time, thinking it wouldn't be suspicious to ask it to a blacksmith.

"You a native born?" the blacksmith asked. Haran shook his head yes, he hated to lie to the man, and he knew they would eventually figure out he wasn't native born, but all he needed to do was see how they trained, then they could leave this place the way they came.

"Ok then, if you come back tomorrow at dawn, there will be a captain or higher here for their weekly supplies, you can talk to him then," the blacksmith said, and Haran thanked him and went on with his way. It was easier than one might think to tell time here, there was a giant water clock in the center of town, and when it reached a new hour, a bell would ring. It grew quite annoying, but it was also extremely useful.

Haran walked through the door when the water clock struck six, the blacksmith he talked to the day before was talking to a tall brown-haired man in his early twenties near the giant forge. He approached the two men, "Good morning sonny, this is the man you want to talk to right here" the blacksmith said.

The man offered his hand out, "The name is Tomas, nice to meet you."

"Haran, and likewise."

"I hear you were looking to join the Lupens," Tomas said as they broke hands.

"Yes, I am low on money, and my wife refuses to work," Haran said in his Herald character.

"Well, you ever use a sword before," Tomas said.

"Actually, I'd prefer an axe, my father is a logger, and I have been carrying an axe all my life, it'd just be more comfortable." As Ray Hawthorn had told him, they grow trees near the farms, and where there are trees, there are always loggers.

"Ahh sure, that would be totally fine, well at midday, meet me for a little training session next to the farms, let's see how good you are," Tomas said.

"Ok, see you then," Haran said as he walked out of the door.

Haran walked to the farms where he saw Tomas. "Follow me," he said as he walked up to the sheer wall of the cavern. He stuck his finger in a tiny hole, just as Ray Hawthorn had done when they first arrived. Just as it had done before, the wall opened up; Haran was still confused how this thing worked. Was it magic?

As if Tomas knew what he was thinking, he said, "No one knows how it works, but apparently the old Lupen builders were extremely skilled, even to the point where we cant even comprehend it." On the other side of the wall was a very impressive training area with multiple arenas and skilled warriors practicing. They walked in and over to a rack of weapons. There were many axes there, but there was only one that looked like his usual one. However, it was very dull, it would probably not even able to cut firewood. He decided not to say anything, even with blunted weapons, he believe he would be able to beat the captain.

You ready to go?" Tomas asked as he went to a free arena.

"Ready when you are," Haran said as he got into his fighting position.

Tomas had a spear and buckler, a deadly combo, especially with only one axe. They circled, Haran knew he would have to negate the range of the weapon Tomas carried, but he had no idea how. For now, he would wait for Tomas to strike first... And he did, with blistering speed, a thrust that Haran parried with ease, he returned with an overhand of his own, but the boy was to far away. . They exchanged a few more times, every time, Tomas slid out of the range of the axe. Haran realized without another axe, he would lose, he will have to nullify the spear's reach.

Then it hit him, the practice spear was all wood, if he could get a clean strike on the shaft, he could break it in half, even with the blunted axe. So, he waited, and waited as they went back and forth, waited for his time to strike. And it came, a thrust came from the spear, but Haran was ready, he shifted his back foot to the left, making his whole body move that way by half a dozen centimeters or so, in turn making the spear miss Haran by half a centimeter. Haran used his free hand to grab the shaft near the head, and with an iron wrist made from throwing thousands of knives, he held it there. He brought the axe high above his head, and with the force of thousands of hours of practice, he hit the shaft, shattering it into millions of tiny pieces.

Immediately, he wheeled the axe around his head straight at Tomas, stopping it only a centimeter from the young man's head.

"Ho- Ho- How do I- kee- losing?" Tomas stuttered in sheer disbelief. The other people there all turned to look at what had just happened.

"UMMM, I have to leave," Haran said as he had just realized what he had done, he had let his head get to him, not wanting to lose, just drew way to much unwanted attention to him.

He ran to the house given to them, opened the door to house to see Lyra tied up to a chair, and three men standing nearby. "Well, hello there old friend, it looks as if you are lost, maybe we can help you," Lottie said as he laughed manically, something hit him in the back of the head, and everything went black.

Chapter 29

———————— ❈ ————————

Haran woke up in a dark, damp room tied to a chair. "Lyra," he croaked, his throat dried from dehydration, but there was no response. So he tried again, "Lyra!"

"She isn't here young man," Doran said as he emerged from the shadows.

"You better not harm her, or I- I will," Haran stuttered to be honest, there was nothing he could do, he was utterly useless.

"You'll what, kill me, and what means do you plan on doing that with," Doran said, scoffing and laughing at the same time.

"Just tell me she's ok, as well as Shiva and Scarlett," Haran said, worried about his pet.

Doran saw the anguish on Haran's face and decided to throw him a bone, though he had few remaining, "The girl is fine, as well as your furry little friends, but for now, I have to know. Why are you here?"

Haran quickly shut his jaw, there was no way he could tell the enemy of their plans. "Ok, I see, a little stubborn are we. Well, how about I get that girl in here, and maybe she will tell me why you two are here. It would be a shame to mess up that pretty face though." Doran said as he made his way to the door.

"Wait," Haran said, he knew that if he shared sensitive information, he would be betraying Orion's trust in him, but they had Lyra, and Orion would never forgive him if he let Lyra die.

So, he told Doran that they had discovered their secret city through Lottie, and that Orion sent them down to see what was going on. Ignoring the part about King Nigel and Cassius, the Outryder Commander.

"That Orion, always a pain in my side without him even realizing it," Doran said.

"So, I have told you everything, do we get to go free," Haran said, hoping for the best.

"You know what, actually yes, wait here," Doran said as he went out of the door. Haran was confused, he had asked that as mostly a joke.

He came back several minutes later with a piece of paper in his hand, "This, is a letter, written by me to be delivered to your master to deliver to the king. It shall only be opened by Nigel himself, and as insurance for this deed being done, we shall keep your pretty little Lyra, and your pretty little pets."

Haran went to protest, then stopped, "How will we get them back," he was seeing this as a plausible option.

"You will just have to find that one out when you deliver it to Nigel himself now won't you," Doran said as he cut Haran from the chair.

He took the note and followed Doran to the tunnel that they had come in with Ray, he hated that he had failed both Lyra and Orion, but this was the only way to rectify that mistake. He had to get out of here, get to Orion, get the letter to the king, and get Lyra back.

As agreed after Haran left the festival early, Heide and Haran were supposed to meet at the start of every month at the castle gates.

"Oh, come on Haran, where are you," she whispered to herself after having waited there for an hour or so. She decided that she would go to Fuestres Woods, which is where Haran had told her he lived and trained.

As she approached the looming forest, she looked for an entrance, eventually finding a small game trail about ten meters off the road. She followed all the twist and turns of the brooding maze passing a strangely cut tree across the path at least ten times until, as she had predicted, "Hands up, state your business," Orion said from behind her, knife in hand ready to be thrown.

She turned around, "Sorry, I was just looking for Haran, we were supposed to meet today, and he didn't show."

"Oh, you must be Heide," Orion said as he sheathed the knife.

"In the flesh, oh and where did you say Haran was again," Heide was a diplomat, she knew how to get things out of people, too bad she was dealing with Orion.

"He is out on a mission," Orion said.

"Without his master?" Heide asked seemingly casually. He flinched slightly, an apprentice should never go anywhere without their master, especially on a mission as dangerous as the one he was currently on.

Before he had time to answer the impossible question, Orion heard a distant sound, a sound he had heard many times before, the sound Haran's footsteps. "Oh, here he is now," he said as he whipped around to see Haran running full speed down the trail.

WACK, he went straight into Orion who didn't even budge from the impact, "Now why would you do that?"

"No time for lectures, we have to get this to the King now," he said as he pulled out the letter. Orion realized what had happened immediately and turned back, heading towards the clearing.

"I am very lost here, what has happened," Heide asked as she ran to catch up.

"Heide no time for questions, they have Lyra," Haran said finally.

Chapter 30

❧

Haran did not have much time for greeting his horse Spirit, he just saddled him up and began preparing for the trip to Anjagor Castle.

"What shall I do Haran," Heide asked, wanting to go with them.

"Hop on or go home, but do it fast," Orion answered her.

She chose the former and got onto Spirit with Haran. They rode in silence until they got out of Fuestres Woods until Orion spoke, "How did this happen Haran?"

"Lottie and Gilpin came back early and apparently they saw us. They knocked me out and took me to a dungeon below the water clock and I don't know where they took Lyra, but they said that if I didn't tell them everything they would harm her, and I just couldn't accept that…" Haran said the words so quickly he had to take a breath.

"Whoa-Whoa-Whoa slow down, you said that Gilpin came back with Lottie and took you and Lyra?" Orion asked.

"Yes, and then a man came in and said you were a pain in his side and let me go to deliver this letter," conveniently ignoring the part where he told Doran how he knew about Randint Cavern.

"But not Lyra," Orion said finally understanding.

"Yes, he said he would keep her, and the only way we could get her back was to give the King the letter," Haran said as he shifted awkwardly on top of Spirit.

"Well why don't we open it and see what we are dealing with," Orion said as he reached for the letter in the saddle pocket.

"NOOO, you can't, he said only the king can open it, or he will harm Lyra," Haran said frantically.

"It's ok Haran, we will get her back," Orion promised him. He put the letter in his saddlebag and went back to riding.

After many hours of riding hard they finally reached the looming bridge, the only way into the castle. Again, they crossed, and again a young guard said, "State your business," then he realized they were Outryders and let them pass by, but this time the guard seemed very hubristic and pompous, as if he were better than the Outryders, but still had to let them pass out of duty.

Orion, noticing his attitude, decided to talk to him a little more, even though they were on a time crunch, "What is your name boy?"

"Terence," the boy said as he met the shorter man's gaze.

"And your parents are," Orion asked again.

"General Lee is my father," Terence said.

"Figures," Orion said as he walked Nova past the boy and onto the castle gates.

There was no Cassius to meet them at the gates this time, so they just led their horses on through to the courtyard. Leaving their horses in the stables, they made their way up to the keep where Orion rapped the door to Nigel's study.

"Coming," Nigel's voice called out from inside. Now is when Cassius appeared, on his way back from a training exercise with a younger Outryder, Theses. The door opened as Cassius rounded the corner of the stairs making a strange call of, "Orion?" in unison.

"Yes, Yes enough pleasantries however, we really must meet in private," Orion said as he gestured to the king's study.

As the five went into the study, Nigel turned to Heide." Pardon. Have we met?"

"No my king, the name is Heide, I am a courier for Norhall Fief," she said very dignified.

"Well, its nice to meet you miss Heide," Nigel said as he kissed her hand.

"Sir, Lyra has been kidnapped," Orion said, Nigel looked up shocked, "And Haran has been set free only to give you this letter," Orion said as he handed the letter to the king.

As King Nigel was taking the letter, Cassius said glaringly, "I warned you that they weren't ready Orion."

"We were ready sir, but Lottie came back three days earlier than we anticipated," Haran interjected, but before Cassius could respond Nigel held up his hand for silence.

He read it,

> *Dear Nigel,*
>
> *It seems as if your ploy of discovering our deepest secrets have failed and I now have an Outryder of yours. If you would like to see her alive again, you will meet me and three of my greatest warriors at Calcore Canyon on the night of the spring equinox along with the boy, the Outryder commander, and the dreaded Orion. How about let us end this thing for good.*
>
> *From- Doran*

"Can we afford to trust him," Cassius asked.

"Can we afford not to," Nigel asked in return.

"Listen, one of my apprentices are in grave danger from a plan that I concocted, I am getting her back with you or without," Orion said.

"How much time do we have," Haran asked, not knowing the date of the equinox.

It was Heide that interjected this time, "We have exactly two weeks from today." They all nodded, realizing how little time they had.

Nigel and Cassius exchange glances, then Nigel spoke, addressing Orion, "We are on board, what's the plan."

Before Orion could reply there was a knock on the door. "Who is it," Nigel said loudly enough for the person to hear.

"General Lee your majesty, may I come in."

"Yes, Yes, we were just finishing up in here," Nigel replied as he opened the door and gestured for the others to exit.

Lee was a big man in his mid-forties dressed in chainmail. Orion could see the resemblance between him and the young man that addressed him so rudely on the bridge. As he thought about it, he decided to speak, "General Lee, respectfully, your son is very abrasive and quite rude."

"Pardon?"

"Your son, Terence I think, is rude, he was bridge guard today and was frankly quite disrespectful, if you could just fix his attitude that would be acceptable," Orion said without even stopping or regretting what he was saying.

"Dually noted," Lee said, he was furious that this wood dweller would even look at him much less admonish his parenting style. But he, being a little smarter than Terence, decided that he would get his revenge some other way.

Sensing the tension, Nigel turned to Lee, "Well, what did you need to talk about," as he led him into his study.

"Oh, my goodness Orion," Cassius laughed as they exited the door and onto the hallway.

"What, do I stink or something?" Orion asked as they went down the stairs to wait for the king to finish speaking with his general Lee.

Chapter 31

❈

Lottie walked into Doran's office around midday; he and Ella had been called in there by Gilpin. They sat as they looked up at the older men, "So, as you both know, we ambushed and captured both of Orion's Recons." The two smiled and gave a little clap then allowed Doran to continue, "However, the boy, Haran, has escaped and killed two guards on his way out."

"HE WHATTT," Lottie flew out of his chair and turn towards the door.

"Where are you going, he is long gone now." said Gilpin.

Lottie realized this and began to settle down a little bit. "Good," Doran said calmly. "Now please listen."

"Yes Sir," Lottie said as he sat back down.

It was Ella who spoke now, almost as furious, "So what do we do now?"

"Well, I assume when the boy reports to his master that they will send a message to me asking to meet them with the girl," Doran said.

"And what do you plan to do when we meet them," Lottie asked.

"We end this for good," Gilpin replied.

Ella walked into the kitchen where she saw her mother setting the table for lunch. "Hey mom," she said as she sat at the table.

"Hey honey, what were you and the boys talking about up there?"

"Oh nothing, they were just saying that Haran escaped and killed two people," Ella replied.

"Oh, that's terrible," Sylvia asked.

"Yeah, to be honest, I don't know why we have to fight like this, Lyra and Haran were always nice to me," Ella said sadly.

"Oh? Well sometimes people are nice to others to gain their trust," her mom said as she took plates from the cabinet above her head.

"Well, yeah I guess, but this actually seemed real, and I hate that Doran is making us fight like this." Ella said, if she were honest with herself, she didn't really have a reason to dislike Doran, but she did.

Sylvia stopped what she was doing, put down the plates and pulled a chair up next to her daughter, "You know, we haven't really got to connect since your father died, and that is all my fault. And I know it must be hard for you to see me happy with Doran, but I ask you nicely, can you please give him a chance." Ella shook her head slightly, ready to respond, but her mother beat her to it.

"One day, that is all I ask of you, one day, just me you and him, and just maybe that Lottie boy you have been goggling overr," and as she said it she saw her daughter beam brighter than she had since her dad was alive.

"Fine, one day, me you Doran AND Lottie," Ella said as she got up from her chair to tell Lottie.

For their day out, they went above ground. The day before they decided that they would make the journey across the border to Osmole fief to meet Ella's grandfather, and Sylvia's dad. It had been almost a year since Ella was sent out looking for her mother, and she really missed her grandfather.

As they rode, Sylvia and Doran side by side, and Ella and Lottie the same a few meters behind, well out of earshot. Ella thought back to the day when she saved Gilpin from bandits on this very road. How it led her to meeting Lottie, and reuniting with her mother, noticing her change in expression, Lottie said, "Is everything ok?"

"Yeah, Yeah, I am fine, I was just thinking that... well you were always so kind to me Lottie, and I trust you with anything, and I was just thinking, do you think Doran is a good man. Good enough for my mother," as she was saying this, she saw her mother laughing ahead.

"Well, from the months I have spent with him, he seems like a great man, and if I am honest, he and Gilpin are some of the best mentors one could ask for, so I don't see why he wouldn't be a good husband as well." Lottie responded, if he were honest, Gilpin and Doran were like father and uncle to him and he liked Doran a lot.

"But, I just don't think he could ever be like my father," Ella said.

"And he doesn't have to be El, he could never replace your actual father, but your mother is happy, and he is making her happy, so what more could you ask for," Lottie said.

"Thank you, Lottie, you are the absolute best," Ella said as she slipped her hand out for Lottie to hold. And they rode hand in hand all the way to Osmole fief.

They reached the Osmole Battleschool around midday, it looked like the Norhall Battleschool but it was just a lot smaller. Gilpin assumed that they would only have 50-75 students there. In the lobby area, they asked an old woman, presumably the receptionist, for Battlemaster Lance, Ella's grandfather. They waited for half an hour in the main office building, before someone came back to them, however it was not him, but it was Sir Regan, an old friend of the family, and right-hand man to the Battlemaster.

The old man looked in his early seventies, grey haired, squared jawed, and blue eyed, Ella recognized him instantly, running over to hug him, "Uncle Regan!!!!"

"Oh my lord Ella, you've gotten so beautiful," Regan said as he lifted her from her feet.

"Hey Reg," Sylvia said as she got up.

"Sylvia is that you, oh my, its been years," Regan said as he went to embrace her as well.

"Yes it has, where is father?" she asked as she looked over his shoulder. And there he was, as healthy as he was the day she left.

"Dad?" He looked like Sir Regan, but his eyes were light green, a signature trait of the Frenger's.

"Sylvia?" he said as he looked at his daughter.

"It's me, and Ella," she said as Regan let them both go.

"Oh my goodness, Ella, my darling, you found her, you found your mother," Lance said as he went to hug them both, and as he did, he saw both Doran and Lottie stand up, "Doran?"

Doran nodded and Sylvia asked, "You two know each other?"

"Of course, why else would I tell you to go to Randint Cavern, I knew Doran would take care of you," Lance said as he broke his embrace from his daughter and granddaughter. "But I have yet to meet him," he said pointing to Lottie.

Lottie offered his hand to the older man, "I'm Lottie Sir, Ella's uhmmm boyfriend."

That made Ella smile a little, he had never said he was her boyfriend before, "Well its nice to meet you Lottie," Lance said as he took the boy's hand, "Well, do yall care to join me for lunch."

"I don't know about what they want to do, but my stomach is definitely nodding yes," Lottie said, leaving the rest to laugh at the joke.

That night, after a day of catching up and talking, Doran walked into Battlemaster Lance's office. The old man was sitting by the fire reading a book called, *Deception, the Key to Victory*, he noticed the entrance and put down the book.

"Hey Lance, its such a shame we have to talk like this," Doran said, he didn't want Sylvia to know of the coming war between the Lupens and Anjagor, so they were forced to meet at this time.

"Yeah, it is, is everything primed for the revolution," Lance asked, he oversaw all of the Lupens in Osmole fief. Many were farmers, blacksmiths and artisans that were scared that the imperialistic expansion of Anjagor would see them killed. Many of these people, including Lance, held Anjagor responsible for the Athonian invasion ten years ago, and all the death and destruction that came with it.

"Everything is set, and once we kill the king, everything else should be in place to take over Norhall, and eventually all of Anjagor," Doran said convincingly.

"How are you so sure this will work," Lance asked, he was very skeptical of Doran's motives, but decided to do whatever it took to get rid of Anjagor.

"Well my father, even though he was a putrid man, was right on one thing, my brother will always want to prove himself the better man, but he has grown lazy in his approach, when I take him out, there will be nothing to stop us." Doran said as he sat down beside Lance to talk business.

Chapter 32

❖

Haran had been training like a madman ever since he got the news that he could get Lyra back. Two words from Doran's letter ran through his mind and kept him going, *greatest warriors,* deep down he knew that Lottie was one of those. He had seen Lottie in action many months ago, and by then, he was already one of the most fearsome warrior Haran had seen. And Haran knew he would have to fight him.

He also knew, that if he were to beat Lottie, he would have to kill him, and he didn't know if he could handle that. So he trained to be good enough to beat him without having to go to such an extreme, sixteen hours a day he practiced with Orion or Cassius or some random castle guard.

A week passed, and even though he felt like a bag of rocks he was starting to see his hard work pay off. He could beat every castle guard with one hand tied behind his back, he could beat Cassius half the time, and even Orion he beat one out of five times. After just getting barely beat by Orion, his master noticed the disappointment on the boy's face, "Haran. Why are you working yourself so hard? Your old skill level could have beat any of the warriors Doran threw at you."

"Not Lottie," Haran replied simply as he went for his water.

Orion figured that what all of this was about, his apprentice had told him of the old rivalry, and he also knew how good Lottie was, "Listen Haran, I know it seems an impossible task to beat him, but if you are too tired to lift your arms to defend yourself next week, then where does that leave you? How does your death help Lyra?" Haran went to protest, but then stopped as he realized his master was right, there was no way he could beat Lottie if he continues this rigorous training.

"I will relax for a few days, but first… How do I beat him if it comes to it?" Haran said, he needed his master's advice if he were to beat Lottie without killing him.

"My boy, you must not fight to beat what is front of you but fight to see the thing you love most the next day," Orion said.

"But what if I don't know who I love," Haran asked conflicted with his feelings for Heide and Lyra.

"Then you shall surely lose." Orion said as he led Haran up to their rooms in Anjagor Castle.

Lyra woke up again in the same stone bed she had been sleeping in for a week, ate the same type of horrible soup she had for a week, and stared at the same four grey walls she had for a week. A man walked in today, the same one that had visited her the first three days, and the same man that had told her that her best friend had abandoned her, Doran. But well after he left the wood door slowly creeped open again and the torch light came pouring in from the hallway outside, something was off, no one was suppose to be visiting her at this time, what time WAS it she thought.

A small, feminine figure appeared, she couldn't recognize anything about them due to the influx of light in the usual dark room, but she recognized the voice that said, "Lyra? Is that really you?"

"Ella." Lyra replied plainly, truthfully, she didn't want to speak to her old friend.

"Yes, how have they been treating you," Ella said sympathetic to her problem.

"About as good as you expect," Lyra said crassly as she began to see Ella more clearly now.

"Hey listen, I know you don't really like me right now, so I pulled a few strings and got you this," she went into the hallway for a minute or so, then came back into the room with a cage, one that held Scarlett.

Lyra's heart jumped as she saw her beloved pet run towards her, "Thank you Ella, but what of Shiva," Lyra was also worried of what had happened to Haran's pet.

"I couldn't get something of that size in here with you, that's liable to cause trouble, but I can assure you, she is being taken care of." Ella said, if she were honest, she didn't know that she would want to deal with getting that big cage all the way to the dungeons. Lyra's head dropped a little bit, so Ella decided to give her the last big surprise, "Oh, and also," she went into the hallway again, walked in and threw two wooden practice axes at Lyra's feet, "you can train now."

"Really?" Lyra was very confused with this one, how could they give her weapons, even if they were wooden.

"Yeah, I figured if you were going to try and fight your way out, you wouldn't get to far with wooden ones." Ella said, but truthfully, Doran said to give those to her as well because, 'If someone doesn't have something to occupy their time, they become dangerous.'

"Thanks Ella, but I need you to tell me something," Lyra said, wanting to know the truth.

"Yeah, what is it?" Ella asked, ready to answer everything she could.

"Did Haran really abandon me?" Lyra asked she was ninety nine percent sure it was a lie, but she had to make sure.

"Umm, to be honest, I don't really know, I feel as if sometimes I am being lied to about you two, because you both seem very nice," Ella said genuinely.

"Thank you, Ella," Lyra said as she was now one hundred percent sure.

"Have a great night Lyra," Ella said as she shut the door behind her, leaving Lyra back in the dim light of the room.

Ella walked into Doran's study soon after she left Lyra's cell. Lottie and Gilpin were already in there but waited for her to arrive before they started. "Welcome Ella," Doran said as she sat down.

"What is it that you called us in here for," she asked ready for sleep.

"The king has replied, apparently he wants to meet us at Calcore Canyon in a week with the girl," Doran said only slightly bending the truth.

"A week? Do you think Haran will be there?" Lottie asked already knowing what he was going to do.

"Most definitely, but if it comes to it, you will surely be able to do the deed," Gilpin said.

"What deed?" Lottie asked, confused by the phrasing.

"Well, we cant quite leave them alive now can we." Doran said as he leaned over the table and looked Lottie right in the eyes.

Chapter 33

❀

Haran walked into the castle stables with Orion at midday to saddle up Spirit. Today was the day that they were supposed to meet at Calcore Canyon to rescue Lyra. He was nervous about having to fight Lottie.

"Orion, do you think I am ready to face him," Haran asked as he thought about his old friend's skill.

"Of course, if anyone can, it's you," Orion said trying to reassure his apprentice.

"Then why do I feel so afraid," Haran said needing to tell someone of what he was feeling.

"Haran, why don't you close you eyes for me," Orion said as he continued saddling Nova. Haran, not understanding, trusted his master and closed his eyes. "Ok now picture the tallest mountain you have ever seen… you are at the bottom of this mountain, you have traveled down the longest road to get to here, but what is here, what is over this mountain? What is the thing you most desire in this world?" Orion said as he saw Haran flinch a little bit.

"To see my parents," Haran said as he thought about what he wanted most.

"Over this mountain is your parents waiting for you to live your life with them as their one and only beloved son. What do you do?" Orion asked as he pulled the saddle strap tight, and nudged his knee in Nova so he let out all the air he just breathed in. These horses were smart, whenever they were getting their saddle put on, they would breath in so the saddle wasn't so tight when they breathed out.

"I climb the mountain to see them," Haran said as he thought about his parents.

"But the mountain is tall, and if you fall you could die." Orion said trying to drive his point across.

"I would hold on tighter until I rose to the top," Haran said.

Orion smiled, got it in one he thought, "Now that you have reached the top, open your eyes." And he did, not necessarily understanding the point.

"Haran, no one should fear being afraid, fear is what drives us to push harder, hold tighter; climb the mountain." Orion said as he saw the boy start to realize. "Courage isn't the absence of fear, it is actually derived from it."

"Thank you, Orion, that's exactly what I needed," Haran said as he held his head up high, the only person who could make him lose, was himself.

"Alright, let's go get Lyra why don't we," Orion said as he led Nova out of the stable and onto the gate where King Nigel and Cassius were waiting for them.

The four men walked to the canyon's edge at sunset, there were no signs of the Lupens which was always a good thing. Orion had a nagging feeling in the back of his mind that they were about to see an army, but to his great relief, there was no army in sight, just rocks and the occasional scurry of a small mouse.

"No signs of them, what if they don't show?" Haran asked worried for Lyra and his pet.

"They'll show." Nigel said hawk eyed and focused on the place where he expected them to come from. He carried a beautifully engraved, strangely shaped sword, it had one edge that curved up. It had a long handle, obviously for two hands, and looked as if it could slice through anything if you put enough power in the blow. He also carried a small knife on his boot, easily accessible if it ever came to it.

After several more minutes, Haran saw the gleam of Lottie's swords off of the fading sunlight, "They're here," he said as he saw four people come from the canyon below.

He caught a glimpse of Lyra tied up carrying one cage with Ella carrying the larger one presumably those of Scarlett and Shiva, respectively. Doran, the man that set him free, led the pack carrying a giant longsword that had to be one and a half to two meters in length. To his right being Gilpin with his sword and buckler and his left Lottie. To Lottie's left, Haran saw the prophesized savior, already standing as tall as the biggest wolf Haran had ever seen after only eight months. The wolf looked as calm, unlike many others of its kind. Had Lottie been able to tame the wolf god?

As the Lupens reached the top of the canyon, they stopped five meters away from the Outryders and the king. The wolf sat at the side of Lottie, patiently waiting for his instructions; how had he done this, Haran thought to himself. He did not even have that kind of control over Shiva.

He saw his poor creature trapped in a cage as he looked over toward her. Her eyes were sad and fierce at the same time, she wished for everything to return to her master, but was stuck in this confining cage. He locked eyes with Lyra whose eyes were as warm as ever, but Haran thought, for different reasons, these eyes were fiery as if she would do anything to get free to be with her best friend again.

"What is it that you want Doran," Nigel said as he broke the silent tension.

"Why do you assume I want something Nigel," Doran said back, trying to keep his ruse up as long as possible.

"That is King Nigel to you, and why else would you take one of my Outryders for hostage, you obviously want something," the king said trying to get the truth out of the man standing across from him.

"Well Nigel, you see, you sent these infidels of yours into my home, you are grateful I didn't kill them on the spot," Doran said bringing up a very valid point.

"So why didn't you, as you said, I sent them down there into the belly of the beast, that means if you didn't kill them, you must need them for something," Nigel said in an excellent phrase of words.

"I like her eyes," Doran said as he shrugged it off.

"You little..." Haran said as he pushed forward slightly only to be stopped by Orion, whose eyes said, not yet.

Noticing the commotion, Doran said, "ahh the little rat I let free, how lovely it is to see you again, tell me, what have your parents been up to these days."

Haran turned angrier than ever before only to be stopped again by Orion, "this isn't your fight, its his," he said as he pointed to the king. Lottie looked up, 'let free', he thought. Doran said Haran had escaped and killed guards, what did he mean, 'let free'.

"DORAN, focus, I already know what you want from me, why don't you just say it," Nigel said as he began to get a little angry.

"Fine, fine fine, you are no fun you know that?" Doran said as if it were a joke, but he was still deadly serious.

"Now, what is it that you want Doran," Nigel said smiling as he had finally got it out of him.

"I want... a Shinoketto brother." Doran said as he began a fighting position.

Chapter 34

❈

A wave of confusion went over everyone in the crowd other than Nigel and not surprisingly Orion. In the confusion they neglected to see Heide approaching on a horse behind them, "What is a Shinoketto?" Haran asked, having heard the name before.

"It is Ushayian for fight to the death," Heide said. Haran remember Orion had told him something of Ushay before, it was a savage culture to the east who invaded Anjagor around forty years ago. They were eventually beat back across the Chien Mountains through a combination of their losses, and their peace treaty with Nigel's father.

"Smart girl," Doran said.

"You are right brother, she is smart; But surely a Shinoketto can be avoided," Nigel said as he didn't want to kill his younger brother.

"Brother? What is happening Doran, what does he mean brother?" Gilpin asked, but Doran said nothing.

Orion who had pieced together the whole thing now spoke up, "Ah, I see, right before he died, King Ferrand, their father, told me the day he appointed me to Norhall. To keep an eye on his lost son. At first, I didn't know what he was talking about, but now I realize, Doran, is the second born son to King Ferrand, he is the 'lost son'."

Doran started laughing uncontrollably, "Of course he called me his lost son, the stupid old bag."

"Don't talk about father like that Doran," Nigel said getting angry of the blatant disrespect to his father.

"Why don't you come and make me." Doran said as he pulled his sword to his chest.

"If I win you let the girl free?" Nigel said, knowing his brother will stick to his word if said out loud.

"Gilpin, if I happen to lose, set the girl and the animals free," Doran said as he took his eyes off of his brother for a second.

Gilpin nodded, and Nigel, having got confirmation, pulled his sword out and to his chest as well, and they circled each other for many of seconds. It was Doran who made the first strike, a deadly overhand cut, that would surely kill anyone standing in the way of it. Luckily, Nigel was not, for he had jumped to his left, narrowly avoiding the blow. They have both kept their swordsmanship sharp since they became leader of their respective countries, not masters as they were in their prime's, but still very excellent. As Nigel rolled to his feet, he threw a short and fast underhand at his brother's right side which was barely parried in time.

As the two continued exchanging blows, Nigel said, "What are you doing this for Doran, father is dead, nature has done what you failed to."

After parrying a deadly side-cut, Doran shouted, "This isn't about you brother, this is about the Lupens, great-grandfather took everything from them, and I won't stop until I make reparations."

Doran went on the offensive now, rage driving his every move, he pushed his brother to the edge of the canyon. Only a meter from the edge, Nigel held his ground, but he couldn't keep that up for long, his brother was delivering blows of such power, that even when parried, they shook Nigel's arms to the bones.

After another minute of parrying, Nigel's arms lost just enough strength for Doran's savage blows to break through. Nigel fell to his knees, clutching his sword for any form of protection, but to no avail, Doran kicked the sword out of the king's hand, and into the canyon below.

"What are you going to do now brother, you have lost; I have bested you this time, and there is nothing that you can do now," Doran said as he leaned closer and grabbed Nigel by the back of the neck.

That was the worst mistake he had ever made in his life, for Nigel had grabbed the small knife from his boot and drove it deep into his younger brother's heart. A small gasp came from Doran as he collapsed upon the ground below, "Oh my... wha-what have I done." Nigel said as he coddled his younger brother's head, frozen by the foul deed he had just done. Doran smiled, he finally got what he wanted in life, for he had broken his brother in his dying breaths.

"Nooooooo," Lottie screamed as he rushed over to the king lying over the dead body of one of his father figures.

He drew his swords as he ran up to the king holding back the tears in his eyes, "How could you!" Rage flew throughout Lottie, he lifted his swords against the grieving king ready come down on the king's grieving body with all his might... but he never reached his destination, for Haran had stopped the blow in its tracks with his axes. "We can't be having that now can we Lottie?" He said as he pushed Lottie's swords away, sending Lottie slightly off balance.

"Haran stay out of this!" Lottie shouted with rage at his old friend.

"They made a deal Lottie, now be a man of your word and hand Lyra over now," Haran said calmly.

Lottie simply laughed, he couldn't even believe what his old friend just said, "No", he said as he switched from laughing to rage again. "And what are you going to do if I don't huh? You going to kill me? Give it your best shot."

Before Haran could make the first move, Heide shouted from behind Haran, "What are you two doing, this is ridiculous. Hasn't there been enough blood shed?"

"Shut up Heide," they said in unison.

"Listen, both of you, I know your angry, but you have to remember, you both used to be the closest of friends. I believe you can again." Heide said not at all offended by their remarks.

Lottie looked around, to the grieving king, to the animals in cages, to the light of the fleeting sun. "Heide" he said as he felt a darkness unlike anything he had ever felt, his mind clouded in a box of darkness he could never get out of. He and Haran were destined for this, and how could he go against his fate. "It was never meant to be," he said as he launched a blistering fast attack at Haran.

As the two boys started fighting, Gilpin decided to sneak behind Haran's back and kill him that way. A knife came flying from his side, landing and inch from his foot, "Don't even think about it," Orion said as he drew his axes and went to attack the Battlemaster. "Cassius, get the girl." He said as he looked to the Outryder commander.

Cassius ran over to Lyra who was being guarded by Ella. "We don't have to fight do we?" she said as she saw him approaching.

"No, just let the girl and animals go and we won't have to," Cassius said, if he were honest, he didn't want to have to fight the girl, she seemed genuinely nice.

"Good, I didn't like having her prisoner anyway," Ella said as she turned to cut off Lyra's bindings and open the animals' cages.

"Thank you," Lyra said as she moved her wrist around for circulation. Ella let Shiva out first, who, so worried for her master, bolted out of her cage and ran to where her master was fighting for his life against Lottie.

Lottie saw the big cat approaching, and fearful what the creature might do while he was fighting Haran, he whistled for Lupe, who had been sitting waiting for orders. Understanding, the wolf got up and ran straight into the side of the lion, catching her off guard, and sending her flying across the hard ground. However, in the distraction of Lottie whistling, Haran managed to knock one of Lottie's swords out of his hands and send it clattering down the canyon. Parrying Lottie's deadly blows would be relatively easy now that Lottie only had one sword. However, Lottie changed hands. Up until now, Lottie had been fighting with his left hand forward, and his right hand in the back to parry any blows. Now, he switched it up, changing to his right hand, the dominate one. Haran was driven even further back, and as he edged towards the canyon's edge, he decided that he needed to act and fast. He caught a glimpse at Lyra who was now looking at their battle with worry, then he clocked it, Contrium, the move Orion taught him that he had practiced with Lyra for days on end. So instead of backing closer to his inevitable doom at the edge, he stood his ground, parrying, waiting for his perfect moment of hesitation from Lottie... The perfect moment to strike... And there it was, a slight faulter in an otherwise perfect offense, a faulter, that Haran capitalized on. As Lottie came down with a slightly slower overhand strike, Haran stopped it dead in its tracks, as he had done hundreds of times before, and without even having to think about it, his right axe came behind Lottie's hilt, and with the pushing and pulling movement, Haran forced Lottie's sword point to his chin. Lottie, shocked by what had just happened couldn't react, he just simply got on his knees, a sign of surrender to his old friend.

Meanwhile, Orion was dealing with Gilpin, a master swordsman and deadly opponent that he didn't take lightly. Even though Gilpin was a master swordsman, Orion was in a different league of his own, he had already cut the Battlemaster in the arm twice, and in the face once. The gracefulness of Orion is almost ghostly, after disarming his shield, Orion push kicked the Battlemaster to the hard rock ground of the canyon's edge. "Sorry Gilpin, but insurrection isn't the best for your chances of my good graces."

After leaving the Battlemaster utterly useless, he decided to look around to see what had happened to his apprentice. Standing over a kneeling Lottie, it seemed as if Haran had beat his rival, but there was still one fierce battle that was taking place. After Shiva got up from where Lupe had sent her flying, she struck back, pouncing on the approaching wolf. After about thirty seconds of upper hand on the wolf, Lupe used his superior strength to get out from the grappling lion's claws. They circled each waiting for the other to pounce; it was Shiva that made the first move, wanting to get the wolf back in the grapple, she tried pouncing again, but this time Lupe was ready. He avoided the lion and pounced on her faster than Shiva could react. They struggled, clawing and biting at each other, neither landing a blow that would end the fight. Until, after Lupe had gotten ahold of Shiva a second time, he held the lion down long enough for him to get a good bite into Shiva's shoulder blade, tearing through the lion's tendons.

Orion watched in horror fifteen meters away as the lion cried in anguish, he sent two knives flying towards the wolf, each landing square on his back, the wolf barely flinched from the pain keeping his jaw locked in the poor lion. Out of the corner of his eye, Orion saw a red figure running full speed at the wolf, and not even a second later, he heard Lyra cry, "SCARLETT, NOOOO!!!"

The fox, trying to save her friend, ran full speed into the wolf knocking the wolf back from Shiva, but not for long. Lupe, angry that this small creature interrupted him, turned his attention to Scarlett, and in one bone chilling crunch of his teeth, the fox died.

"NOOOOO!!!" Haran shouted. "CALL HIM OFF AND WE WILL LET YOU GO," he said to Lottie who was watching his masterpiece come to existence.

Wanting to incite revenge on Haran later, Lottie called the wolf back, "LUPE, come here my beautiful boy," just like that, Lupe stopped his approach to the barely breathing Shiva, and turned towards his master. Ella looked on shocked, wondering how things had escalated so quickly.

"Leave... NOW," Orion shouted at the Lupens.

"We shall get our leader's body first, we need a proper funeral," Gilpin said with a frown on his face, how would they tell Sylvia.

"Get him and go, if you show you faces again, you'll surely end up like him," Orion said trying to ward off any future attempts like these. In vain however, as Gilpin said, "Au contraire."

Chapter 35

❖

Doran's funeral was a beloved one, the whole population came to mourn over the surprising death of their fearless leader; flowers and notes lined the inside of his casket. Sylvia cried in her daughter's arms as she had lost not one but two beloved husbands in her life. Gilpin and Lottie told the tale of his fearsome battle with the king and further reinforced to the masses the atrocities of the Anjagorian government.

Trying to honor the tradition that Doran started, in a couple days, the people of Randint Cavern would cast a democratic vote for who would next lead. However, it would be a redundant affair, for it was a general consensus that the next to lead should surely be Gilpin, Doran's right-hand man, and trusted advisor.

After the nation buried their beloved leader, everyone went home. Everyone except Lottie and Doran, " So, what do we do now?" Lottie asked as he stared at the gravestone that read,

HERE LIES DORAN WERNOCK, FEARLESS LEADER, BELOVED HUSBAND, AND PROUD FATHER.

"Well son," Gilpin said as he turned to Lupe, who was sitting quietly beside Lottie, "I'd say we finished what he started."

Scarlett was buried under the shade of the biggest black oak tree that lined the clearing of Fuestres Woods. A quiet funeral was held for the small animal, with only the six people who had been present when she died. Lyra cried on Haran's arm as they put the box that carried the animal's poor lifeless body into the ground, "I don't understand why Lottie didn't listen to me," Heide kept repeating over and over again, "How could he let this happen?"

However, no one answered, they just stared at the small box in the shallow grave and thought about the things they could have done differently. If Cassius had not let the animals go, none of this would have happened. If Lyra would have stopped Scarlett from running after Shiva, she wouldn't have angered the wolf. If Haran had told Lottie to call off the wolf earlier, he would have prevented it also. If Orion had just thrown his knives at the wolf's heart, he would have surely killed it.

The king was sitting on the porch still visibly shook from having to kill his own brother. Shiva was lying beside him recovering from the devastating wound on her shoulder. After they finished mourning the animal, the small group walked over to the king. "So, what happened with you and your brother all those years ago, why he would want to join the Lupens?" Haran asked Nigel.

The king was still grieving, but he stood and faced his people to tell them the truth, "Doran, was my younger brother, and as all younger brothers are, he wanted to be better than me. However, when it was clear that father was grooming me to take over his place, Doran flew into a rage. He had been born only a year after me, was smarter, and better suited for the position of king, yet as tradition, the first-born son will inherit the throne, and that was me. So he had the brilliant idea to poison both me and my father, however, my plate got switched in the confusion, and he killed an innocent young girl in the process. My father survived for long enough to tell me that Doran had done it, about the Lupens, and to tell Orion here to take care of him, and then he died. Leaving me in charge of Anjagor, and when I was about to arrest him, that's when Doran went to the Lupens. I wiped my brother's name from all the records, told no one of the Lupens and went on with my newfound reign."

As the king finished, everyone now realized why he hadn't told them sooner, Nigel just wanted to protect his brother. "So, what do we do now?" Haran asked to the group with no knowledge that the same thing was being said five kilometers under his feet by his greatest foe, but to this question there was no answer.

Printed in the United States
by Baker & Taylor Publisher Services

Printed in the United States
by Baker & Taylor Publisher Services